U0093847

哈福

哈福

Once upon a time ~

# 英語閱讀滿分特訓

Reading Skill

哇，閱讀英文更簡單了！

最詳盡的作答技巧，英語閱讀實力瞬間 UP! UP!

施銘瑋／主編

Craig Sorenson ／著

林靜慧／譯

哈福

# 六十分鐘滿分特訓・英語閱讀All Pass！

**提升「New TOEIC、iBT TOEFL、IELT、會考、統測、全民英檢」應試實力！閱讀功力一次累積，讓您考試時信心滿滿，不再怯場！**

因應各種考試，英語聽、説、讀、寫四大基本能力已被廣為重視。學英語，除了要多讀多看，字彙累積更是其中一項大工程。各種的英語檢定考試，閱讀測驗都可説是得分焦點，要勝過別人，除了口説與聽力功夫要紮實，閱讀的功力更得爐火純青。為了專攻閱讀，讓自己實力大進級，只要六十分鐘，您準備好了嗎？

特聘外籍老師為讀者編撰的「英語閱讀滿分特訓」，內容包括字彙和結構、段落填空與閱讀理解三部分。

1. **字彙和結構**：五十小題最強力字彙結構特訓，訓練讀者爭取時間，快速搶答的臨場應變實力。

2. **段落填空**：五篇常考短篇文章，針對學習英文者對動詞時態、介系詞選擇的弱點，單刀直入加強訓練。習慣這類問題與答題技巧後，通過英檢勢在必得！

3. **閱讀理解**：包括七則精彩文章，內容多元、有趣，富啟發與專業性，並針對各英語閱讀測驗常考的問法、主題、方向歸納精編測驗題，重點清晰有條理，道道精選考題讓您英檢閱讀測驗輕鬆得高分！

本閱讀特訓特別收錄答題技巧大公開與詳盡的解答分析，更特別編整文章總複習附錄，並附贈閱讀總複習MP3，絕對是您增進閱讀實力的最大秘密武器。跟著六十分鐘的反覆磨練，閱讀能力絕對過人！

本書除精選嚴製題型外，更附上最詳盡的應試小秘訣，所有應考訣竅毫無保留完整大公開！

**解答與分析部分**：特別精心整理的解答範例區，除了提供答題技巧與實用範例補充外，更將文章重點突顯出來，讓您省略畫重點的步驟，閱讀重點一目瞭然！

**重點總整理**：特別編整的重點總整理區，將書中所有的例句與文章統整收錄，並附贈專業外籍老師錄製的高品質MP3一片，讓讀者耳濡目染，快速熟記所有文章與重要單字片語！

六十分鐘快、狠、準的閱讀測驗考題，題型綜合詞彙和結構、段落填空、閱讀理解三部分。附贈專業錄製的高品質MP3，內容完整詳實。藉由書與MP3的雙重火力，讀者除了可以反覆培養考試臨場感，也可以無限次複習標準文章範例，從中培養語感，實力進步快速又有效率！

編者 謹識

目錄
CONTENTS

## Chapter 3

## Answers and Analyses 解答 & 解析



## Chapter 4

## Chapter 5

## Appendix 附錄

## Note 這句英文，改變你的人生

- Pursuits become habits.
  （因循會變成習慣。）
- When sorrow is asleep, wake it not.
  （傷心舊事別重提。）
- Respect yourself, or no one else will respect you.
  （人必先自重，而後人重之。）

Chapter

# Reading Skill

# 閱讀應試秘笈

Welcome and congratulations! You've purchased a book that will help you improve your English and help you score better on English tests. You've probably already studied English for several years now.

This book is designed to help you review and reinforce the English you already know, and at the same time it will also increase your knowledge of vocabulary, grammar, and reading skills.

Before you begin, let's go over a few points that will help you use your studying time more efficiently. Because, as always, it's better to study smarter than to only study harder or longer!

A friend of the famous Roman Julius Caesar once said, "Practice is the best of all instructors." What did he mean by this? With the correct kind of practice, you can be your own best teacher!

Here are a few valuable points to help you practice English better, and make the most of your time studying

歡迎！恭喜你買了這本可以幫助你增進英文能力，且能讓你在測驗中得到高分的工具書。到目前為止，你應該已經讀了好幾年的英文了。

這本書的設計就是要幫助你自我評量並加強你的英文能力，同時讓你提升字彙、文法以及閱讀技巧。

在你開始讀這本書之前，讓我們先討論幾個能夠幫助你善用學習時間的要點；因為聰明地學習，總是比投入更多心力或時間學習要好得多！

著名的羅馬凱撒大帝的一位朋友說過：「練習是最好的老師。」他這麼說是什麼意思呢？這就是說，如果練習得當，你可以做自己最好的老師！

這裡有幾個相當寶貴的觀念可以幫你更有效地練習英語，並且達到最事半功倍的效果。

English.

* Keep learning new words, and keep reviewing the old ones: The reading sections of English tests require you to have a large vocabulary. There are many different ways to learn new vocabulary and you may already know which ways work best for you.

If you have trouble remembering new words, think about this method. Teachers have for many years told students that an effective way to remember new words is to think of clues that you can associate with the word's meaning. Then, whenever you see the word, you will see the clue and remember its meaning. Here's an example: the word 'caterwaul' means: to make a loud screeching, crying sound.

The first three letters of this word are 'c-a-t' or 'cat'. And, as we all know, cats sometimes also make loud screeching, crying sounds.

If you think of this clue, it will help you to remember the meaning of this word every time you see it. Once you practice using this technique, you'll find that it works almost automatically!

＊ **持續學習新字，並複習舊的單字：**做閱讀測驗時，豐富的英語字彙對你而言是相當重要的。而增加字彙有很多不同的方法，你也許已經找到適合自己的方式。

如果你總是記不起新單字，不妨試試以下這個方法，這個方法是許多老師沿用多年的妙招——運用聯想提示記憶法來記誦單字。之後，不管你在何時看到這個字，你都會記得它的提示而想起它的意思。這裡有一個例子：「caterwaul」這個字表示——發出大聲且尖銳、刺耳的嚎叫聲。

這個字的前三個字母是“c-a-t”也就是「貓」的英文單字。我們都知道，貓有時候會發出大聲且尖銳、刺耳的嚎叫聲。

如果你記得這個提示，它就可以讓你在每次看到這個字的時候，想起它的意思。一旦你經常練習這個技巧，你會發現這種方法幾乎可以自動在你的腦中運作！

* Learn for yourself what is your best time, your best place, and your best way to study: Not everyone responds the same to the same environs. Different people learn best under different circumstances and you must find what's best for you.
If you discover that you don't study well early in the morning, then don't waste your time studying early in the morning!

* Spend a little time studying every day: And lastly, a rule that you've heard before: It is much better to spend little time studying every day than to study for a long time once every few days. Some students try to ignore this rule, because they find it inconvenient to study every day.
But if you can find the time and make a habit of practicing English for even 30 minutes a day, then you' will improve faster, and remember more, than if you spendpractice for several hours only two or three days a week.

So keep these tips in mind as you go through this book, and we promise that you'll become your own best teacher.

＊**了解自己唸書的最有效率的時間、地點與方式**：每一個人對同一種環境都有不同的反應；不同的人，學習效率最好的環境也都不同，而你必須知道什麼樣的環境對自己最好。
如果你發現你一大早的學習狀況不佳，那就不要把早上的時間浪費在唸書上！

＊**每天花一點時間讀書**：最後，有一條規則是你曾經聽過的：每天花一點時間讀書的效果，比隔幾天再花一段很長的時間要來得好。一些學生忽略了這個規則，因為他們覺得每天唸書不方便。
但是，如果你能找出時間並養成每天花三十分鐘練習英文的習慣，那你會進步得更快，記得的東西也比較多。這比你一個星期一次花好幾個小時唸書的效果要顯著。

當你在研讀這本書的時候，請記住這些秘訣。我們保證你一定可以成為自己最好的老師。

## Note 這句英文，改變你的人生

- The more noble, the more humble.
  （人愈高尚，愈謙虛。）

- Kindness is the noblest weapon to conquer with.
  （仁愛乃最高貴的兵器。）

- Obedience is the first duty of a soldier.
  （軍人以服從為天職。）

Chapter

# The Test is Coming!

## 測驗題庫

Part 1

## Vocabulary Selection

____ 1. It was only because his car is ____ that he won the race.

A. fasting B. faster
C. slowing D. slower

____ 2. We could finish this homework much quicker if the teacher would let us ____ on it at school.

A. play B. take
C. work D. bring

____ 3. When Joe found that his wife wasn't in the kitchen, he went to the ____ to look for her.

A. lamp B. jewelers
C. aunt D. bedroom



Answer see page 78

____ 4. We ask the other students to _____ our team so that we'll have more people and work faster.

A. jump B. beg
C. join D. borrow



____ 5. He couldn't see the monkey in the tree because it was directly _____ his head.

A. about B. above
C. at D. around

____ 6. The only way to get to the other side of the river is to cross the _____ at the end of the road.

A. building B. bridge
C. bakery D. barbecue

____ 7. The doctor immediately _____ to help the injured man.

A. reviewed B. required
C. rushed D. rescued

Answer see page 78

____ 8. He's been working for eleven months without a _____, I think he should take some time off.

A. vacation B. vagrant

C. vaccination D. vacancy

____ 9. It took us two hours of searching to find his car keys which were _____ his car seat.

A. around B. within

C. about D. under

____ 10. _____ you study every day will you succeed in school.

A. Only if B. Also

C. While in D. Around then

____ 11. His computer stopped working only because the _____ had no power left.

A. battalions B. conscripts

C. batteries D. connections



Answer see page 79

____ 12. His _____ dog followed him around everywhere he went.

A. faithful B. removed

C. perfunctory D. maintained

____ 13. _____ he is from France, he can speak excellent English and Japanese.

A. In order B. Although

C. Before D. Instead

____ 14. The bank has installed many new cameras to improve _____.

A. security B. profession

C. interest D. wisdom

____ 15. I _____ that you fully understand the ideas in the book before you begin criticizing it.

A. entertain B. suggest

C. critique D. testify



Answer see page 79

____ 16. If you want to go up to that village, then you must first climb the ____.

A. river B. mountain
C. plain D. delta

____ 17. The boss gave ____ instructions to his secretary to finish the project this week.

A. inevitable B. specific
C. passive D. displeased

____ 18. Of all of my ____, Sarah is the only one who forgets to do her homework.

A. schools B. campuses
C. classmates D. libraries

____ 19. While the boy was talking to his sister, his sandwich ____ by a bird.

A. stolen B. was stolen
C. steal D. stole



Answer see page 80

____ 20. The politician went into the town to ask the people to ____ for him.

A. vote B. test
C. explain D. govern

____ 21. Some people from the United States find it difficult to eat with ____ when they first go to Asia.

A. calendars B. coupons
C. chopsticks D. cards

____ 22. I'm sorry but I'm too busy tonight, can we meet in the ____ instead?

A. afterwards B. afterthought
C. after D. afternoon

____ 23. The doctor spent twenty minutes ____ the sick girl before he gave her medicine and told her to go home and rest.

A. explaining B. expecting
C. examining D. extraditing



Answer see page 81

____ 24. Wow, have you heard the ____? Sally and Jeff are getting married!

A. news B. scene

C. trial D. measure

____ 25. The best way to ____ health problems is to exercise often and eat a healthy diet with lots of many fruits and vegetables.

A. prevent B. attain

C. preserve D. ascertain

____ 26. Because the singer gives great performances every time, most fans agree that she is very ____.

A. conscription B. contiguous

C. consistent D. complex

____ 27. The movie star was very concerned about his ____, so he was always careful about what he said to the newspapers.

A. image B. inspection

C. fascination D. ambition



Answer see page 81

____ 28. I would like to help you, but I am simply _____ of moving those big rocks.

A. unable B. incapable
C. questionable D. expectable

____ 29. Because our team has had so many delays, it is _____ that we will finish on time.

A. doubtful B. dumfounded
C. definite D. destined

____ 30. People say that drinking tea is better for your health than drinking _____.

A. cylinders B. fedoras
C. coffee D. hills

____ 31. The boy's mother tries to _____ him from spending too much time playing computer games.

A. support B. discourage
C. convince D. encourage



Answer see page 82

____ 32. There's too much ____ in the street so I can't hear what you're saying.

A. noise B. crime
C. people D. stone

____ 33. She's so hungry right now that you can hear her ____ making sounds.

A. shoulder B. stomach
C. septum D. sternum

____ 34. Her most ____ belonging is the book of pictures given to her by her grandmother.

A. difficult B. precious
C. accurate D. entire

____ 35. It ____ more fun if we could have all gone to see the movie together.

A. will be B. was
C. would have been D. was having



Answer see page 83

____ 36. My friend got a job in a computer store because he wanted to learn how to ________ broken computers.

A. perform B. alleviate
C. repair D. complicate

____ 37. The only bad _____ that he has is that he smokes cigarettes.

A. question B. habit
C. talent D. expectation

____ 38. His house is in a great _____, it's right in the middle of the city.

A. message B. location
C. attempt D. penmanship

____ 39. Even if we can't read all of these books, ________ we'll be able to read some of them.

A. all B. at least
C. always D. if all



Answer see page 84

____ 40. The girl ran in and ____ told her friends about finding some money on the street.

A. excitedly B. expectantly
C. professionally D. boringly

____ 41. People expect that better ____ will make their lives easier and more productive.

A. forestry B. biology
C. technology D. chemistry

____ 42. We hope that you will find your lost wallet without too many ____.

A. decisions B. difficulties
C. mentions D. mistakes

____ 43. Only after a long discussion were the boyfriend and girlfriend able to ____ their problem.

A. underscore B. perform
C. utilize D. resolve



Answer see page 84

____ 44. The artist's _____ kept him from ever making money selling his expensive paintings.

A. greed B. talent
C. performance D. usefulness

____ 45. The policeman thought that the fire was _________ started by a dangerous criminal.

A. deliberately B. perfectly
C. usually D. expectantly

____ 46. My friend likes to read _____ more than newspapers.

A. magazines B. microwaves
C. messengers D. miscreants

____ 47. It _____ by the group that they should wait until tomorrow to have the meeting.

A. decide B. was decided
C. decision D. decided



Answer see page 85

____ 48. The teachers all ____ that the best way to learn to speak English is to study abroad.

A. agreed B. agreement
C. agreeing D. agreeable

____ 49. They ____ down the street when they noticed that it was starting to rain.

A. walk B. will walk
C. walking D. were walking

____ 50. The little boy is known for ____ every little story he tells.

A. exaggerating B. supposing
C. convincing D. wasting



Answer see page 86

Part 2

# Cloze Section



## 1

Many young people enjoy ____1____ sports. Basketball is one sport very ____2____ with young people, ____3____ boys. Many boys play ____4____ of basketball while in high school, some even play for their school's basketball ____5____. Because they practice ____6____, some of them get ____7____ very good at basketball. Some of these basketball ____8____ even hope to play professionally someday. But it's very difficult to ____9____ a professional basketball player, and very few of those who try ever ____10____.

Answer see page 88

____ 1. A. player
B. playing
C. play
D. played

____ 2. A. excited
B. famous
C. popular
D. fun

____ 3. A. also
B. especially
C. without
D. for

____ 4. A. lot
B. many
C. a lot
D. much

____ 5. A. team
B. group
C. division
D. unit

____ 6. A. quickly
B. often
C. usually
D. only

____ 7. A. to be
B. are
C. be
D. is

____ 8. A. play
B. player
C. players
D. playing

____ 9. A. change
B. become
C. attest
D. decide

____ 10. A. succeed
B. successful
C. success
D. succeeding


Answer see page 89

## 2

People ____1____ the world use many different methods to build houses. Those who live in areas with forests and many trees often build their homes out of wood, because it's most ____2____. People who live in areas where there are no trees must find ____3____ materials with which to build. For ____4____, people who live in desert areas often use rocks or clay to build houses, ____5____ those who live in jungle areas often use wood and leaves. People are very ____6____, and have used many other things to provide shelter. When wood, rocks and clay are not easily ____7____, then people use a ____8____ of other materials. People in cities use brick and ____9____ to make buildings, while the Inuit of the snowy arctic ____10____ use only snow!



Answer see page 90

____ 1. A. about
B. above
C. around
D. along

____ 2. A. destroyed
B. available
C. sympathetic
D. terrified

____ 3. A. other
B. equal
C. uniform
D. certain

____ 4. A. argument
B. sake
C. example
D. reasons

____ 5. A. which
B. while
C. without
D. whence

____ 6. A. resourceful
B. irritating
C. wise
D. expendable

____ 7. A. forgotten
B. expensive
C. found
D. enjoyed

____ 8. A. system
B. variety
C. class
D. tempest

____ 9. A. fabric
B. steel
C. tempo
D. patent

____ 10. A. dilemmas
B. experts
C. regions
D. attitudes



Answer see page 91

## 3

Sharks are ___1___ of the most ___2___ animals on the planet. For ___3___ as mankind has known about sharks, they ___4___ feared. But actually, sharks pose very little ___5___ to most people. Sharks usually stay away from humans, and ___6___ very rarely swim near beaches or other areas with many people. Many scientists ___7___ that when sharks do attack people , it's is only because the sharks have ___8___ the person for another animal, like a seal. There have been many movies made ___9___ sharks, and most show sharks as being vicious and dangerous creatures. But in ___10___, sharks kill very few people, and overall mankind benefits from their presence in the oceans.



Answer see page 92

_____ 1. A. many
B. some
C. especially
D. one

_____ 2. A. feared
B. helpless
C. expectant
D. alleged

_____ 3. A. as in
B. as long
C. as for
D. as if

_____ 4. A. been
B. have been
C. will be
D. was

_____ 5. A. threat
B. excuse
C. trouble
D. question

_____ 6. A. always
B. only
C. then
D. askew

_____ 7. A. research
B. experiment
C. believe
D. portray

_____ 8. A. mistaken
B. convinced
C. expected
D. attained

_____ 9. A. for
B. about
C. within
D. while

_____ 10. A. real
B. realistic
C. realism
D. reality



Answer see page 93

# 4

Do you believe ___1___ ghosts? Many people ___2___ that because science hasn't proven that ghosts are real, then they cannot be real. These people say that because ___3___ are not any machines or scientific instruments that can help us find ghosts, then they must not be real. But other people have different ___4___. These people say that ___5___ science can't prove ghosts are real, science ___6___ cannot prove that ghosts are not real. So there really are two ___7___ to this argument. This is an issue that in the future may never ___8___. But what do you ___9___? Have you ___10___ seen a ghost?



Answer see page 94

____ 1. A. of
B. in
C. on
D. at

____ 2. A. say
B. saying
C. said
D. says

____ 3. A. this
B. those
C. there
D. then

____ 4. A. opinions
B. requirements
C. uses
D. terms

____ 5. A. already
B. always
C. altogether
D. although

____ 6. A. also
B. and
C. but
D. for

____ 7. A. people
B. sides
C. places
D. machines

____ 8. A. will resolve
B. be resolved
C. resolving
D. have resolved

____ 9. A. think
B. thought
C. thinking
D. will think

____ 10. A. always
B. evenly
C. but
D. ever



Answer see page 95

## 5

Christopher Columbus is one of the most ___1___ explorers in Western history. He was the ___2___ European to sail to the Americas. However, he made many mistakes along the way. First of all, he ___3___ he had arrived in India when he had actually arrived in the central American ___4___. For this ___5___, he called the people of Central America 'Indians'. Also, he got lost ___6___ the times. Back in the 15th ___7___, sailors used the stars to steer their ships. Some sailors were very good at this, but Columbus was not. ___8___ one occasion, he used the stars to calculate that he ___9___ near a certain island in the Caribbean, when actually ___10___ was over two thousand kilometers away!



Answer see page 96

_____ 1. A. perfect
B. famous
C. useful
D. efficient

_____ 2. A. first
B. begin
C. former
D. start

_____ 3. A. think
B. thinking
C. thought
D. will think

_____ 4. A. place
B. country
C. citizen
D. region

_____ 5. A. reason
B. motive
C. alibi
D. excuse

_____ 6. A. one
B. many
C. all
D. each

_____ 7. A. time
B. century
C. week
D. hour

_____ 8. A. At
B. On
C. Of
D. Or

_____ 9. A. were
B. is
C. was
D. are

_____ 10. A. she
B. they
C. we
D. he



Answer see page 97

Part 3

# Reading Comprehension Section

## 1

I had a very good vacation this summer. In June, just when our school vacation began, my family and I went to Newburyport to visit my grandmother and grandfather. Newburyport is a small town near the ocean. My grandparents have lived there for many years, but it's far from my home, so we can only go to see them a few times each year.

We had a great time with my grandparents. One day we went to the beach and found many seashells and also had fun flying a kite. The next day, my grandfather took my brother and me out in his sailboat. Wow! Sailing is so much fun and my grandfather is a very good sailor. The day after that, we went to a



Answer see page 99

nearby lake to go fishing. My brother caught two big fish, but I didn't catch any. We took the fish home and my grandmother cooked them for dinner. They were delicious!

When we got back from Newburyport, my brother and I went to a summer camp. We stayed there for five days. Every day we did many fun things. We played games, went swimming, told stories, went on walks through the woods, and at night we always had big campfires. This was a very fun summer vacation for me! I hope that my next vacation will be as much fun as this one!

* * * * * * * * * * *

____ 1. Which is the best title for this girl's essay?

A. Why my grandparents live in Newburyport?

B. What I did on my summer vacation?

C. Why I like my brother so much?


Answer see page 100

D. Who I saw on my summer vacation?

____ 2. Which of the following is the correct order of events for her summer vacation?

A. First she went to Newburyport, then went sailing, then went to summer camp.

B. First she went to summer camp, then went sailing, then went to see her grandparents.

C. First she went fishing, then went sailing, then she went to Newburyport.

D. First she went to Newburyport, then she went to summer camp, then she went sailing.

____ 3. Which of the following is not something she did while at summer camp?

A. swimming

B. walking

C. bicycling

D. telling stories

Answer see page 100

____ 4. Where does the girl say she flew a kite?

A. She flew a kite at summer camp.

B. She flew a kite at the beach.

C. She flew a kite at summer camp and at the beach.

D. She did not fly a kite.



Answer see page 100

## 2

Dear Lee Qin,

Do you remember me? I'm your old friend James Lee. I haven't written a letter to you in a long time, so I'd like to let you know what I've been doing recently. For the last two years I have been living in the Canadian city of Vancouver. The first year I was here, I was studying English and English literature at the University of Vancouver. It's a very good school and studying there improved my English a lot. When I first arrived in Canada, I found it difficult to communicate with people in English, but now it's no problem.

Most recently, I have been working in an Italian restaurant in downtown Vancouver. My job is to make different kinds of soup and salad. It's a fun



Answer see page 101

job because I get to learn a lot about Italian cooking, and the people I work with are all very nice to me. I only work four days of every week, so I have enough time off to go sightseeing and exploring around Vancouver.

Vancouver is a large city on the West coast of Canada. It's a really beautiful city with many parks, mountains, and even a beach! In the ocean near Vancouver are many islands. I've been to some of them and they're full of natural beauty. All in all, Vancouver is an excellent place and I,m very happy I decided to come here. If you ever feel like coming to Canada, please let me know, because I'd be very happy for you to come visit.

Your Friend,
James Lee



Answer see page 101

____ 1. Who are James Lee and Lee Qin?

A. They are friends from a long time ago.

B. They are students at the same school.

C. They both work at the same restaurant.

D. They are people who don't know each other.

____ 2. According to the letter, when was the last time James Lee wrote to Lee Qin?

A. a few days ago

B. a long time ago

C. never before

D. last week

____ 3. For how long has James been living in Vancouver?

A. One year

B. Two years

C. Three years

D. Four years



Answer see page 102

____ 4. What did James say about the time when he first arrived in Canada?

A. He said that he spoke English very well.

B. He said that he never spoke English.

C. He said that he was only speaking Italian.

D. He said that it was difficult to communicate in English.

____ 5. How did James improve his English skills?

A. He practiced listening to English television shows.

B. He went to a university to study English and English literature.

C. He worked in many different English-speaking restaurants.

D. His English has always been very good and need not improve.



Answer see page 102

____ 6. Does James enjoy his job? Why or why not?

A. He doesn't enjoy his job because it is very difficult and he needs to work every day.

B. He does enjoy his job because he gets to eat a lot of Italian food for free.

C. He doesn't enjoy his job because the people he works with are not nice people.

D. He does enjoy his job because he gets to learn about Italian cooking.

____ 7. What does James say at the end of his letter?

A. He says that he is sorry that he moved to Vancouver because it is not a nice city and he has to work very hard.

B. He says that although Vancouver is a nice city, he wants to move to the United States and go to school.

C. He says that Vancouver was a nice city before, but now it is too crowded and he wants to go to another place.

D. He says that he is very happy that he lives in Vancouver and he would like it if his friend could come to visit.



Answer see page 103

## 3

This Saturday afternoon from 1 pm until 10 PM there will be a Carnival Fun Fair held at the Hillsboro Elementary School on Parker Street in downtown Hillsboro. The fair will include many games, lots of different food to eat, a musical show, as well as many prizes for participants to win.

There will also be a large barbecue cookout beginning at 6 PM and ending when the food is gone! Hamburgers, hot dogs, salad and drinks will all be served free to those who purchase a Carnival Fun Fair entrance ticket. Also the Elvis Rock and Roll Band will give a musical performance beginning at 8 pm and ending when the carnival closes. This performance is also free to all who purchase a Fun Fair ticket.



Answer see page 104

Tickets for the Carnival Fun Fair cost 5 dollars for adults and 3 dollars for children. All of the money made with the fair will be given to the Hillsboro Elementary School library to purchase new books and a computer. So we hope you can all come out this Saturday for a great time at the Carnival Fun Fair, and also support the Hillsboro Elementary School library. See you there!



Answer see page 104

____ 1. Which of the following is the best title for this article?

A. Elvis Rock and Roll Band has recorded a new album.

B. Barbecue will have hamburgers, hot dogs and salad.

C. Hillsboro Elementary School has very funny students.

D. Carnival Fun Fair at Hillsboro Elementary School.

____ 2. Which of the following is true about the Carnival Fun Fair?

A. It will have music and games but will not have any food.

B. It will have music, games and a barbecue.

C. It will only have food and games, and will not have any music.

D. It will have many books and computers to use.



Answer see page 105

____ 3. Which of the following is true about the Carnival Fun Fair?

A. If you purchase a ticket for the fair, then you can go to the barbecue and the Elvis Rock and Roll Band concert for free.

B. If you purchase a ticket for the fair, you will need to buy extra tickets for the barbecue and the Elvis Rock and Roll Band.

C. If you purchase a ticket for the barbecue, then you can also go to the fair and the Elvis Rock and Roll Band concert for free.

D. If you purchase a ticket for the Elvis Rock and Roll Band, then you can go to the fair for free.



Answer see page 105

____ 4. Why is the Hillsboro Elementary School having the Carnival Fun Fair?

A. They want their students to learn about rock and roll music.

B. They will use the money from selling tickets to buy things for the school library.

C. They like to do fun things like having barbecues and playing games.

D. They need to sell many tickets in order to pay for the cost of the barbecue.



Answer see page 106

## 4

Dear Mr. Thomas,

How are you? I am not doing very well myself. Do you remember the camera that you let me borrow? Well, I'm sorry to say that there was a little problem and I lost it. Of course, I would like to pay you so that you can buy a new camera, but first I'd like to tell you how I lost it.

Last Friday, the day you lent your camera to me, I went to the beach to look around. It was a nice day, although a little windy. I was walking down the beach taking pictures when I saw a man in a small boat. The man started talking to me and asked if I would like to go for a boat ride. So I went with him on a short ride.



Answer see page 107

After about twenty minutes, the sun started to set. The sky was orange and red and looked very beautiful. I started to take a picture of the sunset when suddenly a big wave came and hit our little boat! Your camera fell out of my hands into the water, where it sank like a rock. I felt so bad, there was nothing I could do!

So, I am very sorry about losing your camera. I hope you understand that this was an accident. But anyway, please let me know how much it will cost to buy a new one and I'll give you the money at once. I hope that you'll forgive me for this!

Many Apologies,
Jeff Davies



Answer see page 107

____ 1. Why did Jeff Davies write this letter?

A. He wrote the letter because he wants to borrow Mr. Thomas's camera.

B. He wrote the letter to tell Mr. Thomas that he lost the camera he borrowed.

C. He wrote the letter because Mr. Thomas wants to borrow his camera.

D. He wrote the letter because he wants to find Mr. Thomas's camera.

____ 2. Which words best describe the feeling or tone of Jeff Davies's letter?

A. It is angry and upset.

B. It is funny and happy.

C. It is sorry and apologetic.

D. It is rude and demanding.



Answer see page 108

____ 3. Which of the following shows the correct order of events in the letter?

A. Jeff borrowed the camera, then he lost it, then he went for a boat ride.

B. Jeff went for a boat ride, then he borrowed the camera, then he lost the it.

C. Jeff lost the camera, then he went to the beach, then he went for a boat ride.

D. Jeff borrowed the camera, then he went for a boat ride, then he lost the camera.

____ 4. What does Jeff offer to do?

A. He says that he will never borrow Mr. Thomas's camera again.

B. He says that he will give Mr. Thomas money to buy a new camera.

C. He says that he will lend his camera to Mr. Thomas.

D. He says that Mr. Thomas should not be so careless with his cameras.



Answer see page 108

## 5

Most people know that Americans love cars. Of course, this was not always the case. Up until the 1950s, most Americans relied mainly on trains and busses for transportation. This was because at that time, the average American thought cars were too expensive to buy, maintain, and repair. But this all changed in the 1950s and there are several reasons why.

World War II ended in 1945 and began a time of industrial growth in America. There were many factories and machines left over from the war, and these were changed to create new products. Engineers and factory workers who had experience making weapons during the war started making products for the average American. One thing they started making was cars, and they made them cheaper and better than ever before.



Answer see page 109

Soon many more Americans were buying the cheaper cars and this caught the government's attention. The government realized that the country needed more and better roads and highways. For many years during the 1950s, the government spent a lot of tax money building new highways to connect all the states, from East to West and North to South. And once Americans saw all these new roads, what did they do? They bought more cars!

Now it is more than fifty years later, and Americans are starting to learn that too many cars on the roads can cause problems. In most cities in America there are too many cars on the roads, and the traffic moves very slowly. Also, cars cause a lot of air pollution, and people are beginning to worry about how this affects environment. For these reasons, many Americans are choosing not to drive cars. So what are they doing instead? They're using trains and busses again!



Answer see page 109

____ 1. Which of the following is the best title for this essay?

A. Trains and Busses are Better than Cars.

B. World War II and American Roads.

C. A Short History of Cars in America.

D. Cars are Bad for Environment.

____ 2. Before the 1950s, why did few Americans own cars?

A. Because cars were too expensive to buy and maintain.

B. Because cars made too much air pollution.

C. Because the factories that made cars were busy.

D. Because most Americans did not know how to drive.

____ 3. How did the end of World War II affect the production of cars in America?

A. When the war ended, many more people had free time to learn how to make their own cars.



Answer see page 110

B. After the war, many factories and machines were changed to make new products like cars.

C. When the war ended, nobody wanted to make cars anymore so they continued to make weapons.

D. The end of the war made many people realize that machines and technology are not beneficial.

____ 4. What did the government do when it realized that many Americans were buying cars?

A. The government began to look for ways to fix the problems of city traffic and environmental pollution.

B. The government decided that cars were becoming too expensive so they made car companies sell cars cheaper.

C. The government started to build more new roads to connect all parts of the country.

D. The government let people ride on busses and trains without paying money.



Answer see page 110

____ 5. What are some of the problems of having too many cars in America?

A. They create unemployment and poverty.

B. They create pollution and traffic.

C. They create problems for factories.

D. They create more and better roads.

____ 6. According to the essay, what have some Americans started to do because of the problems created by too many cars?

A. They have returned to using busses and trains for transportation.

B. They have asked the government to stop building new roads.

C. They have sold their cars and bought bicycles.

D. They have learned how to repair their cars themselves.



Answer see page 111

## 6

Dear Mr. And Mrs. Lee,

Thank you for your interest in our Tour of America travel package. I would like to give you some more information about our tour and then you will see for yourself why ours is better than the tours offered by other companies.

First of all, our tour takes you to five American cities, while most other tour groups only visit two or three. Our tour will begin in San Francisco in California, then we'll go to Austin, Texas. After two days there, we will travel down to New Orleans in the southern state of Louisiana. From Louisiana, we will go north to the wonderful city of New York. Here you'll get to spend four days shopping, going to museums, and sightseeing around town. Finally, we will go to the midwestern city of Chicago, also known as the "Windy City." If you go with a different company, they would only take you to two or three of these places!


Answer see page 112

The second big advantage of our Tour of America is its size. We limit the size of our travel groups to fifteen people. Why is this? This is so our tour guides can give you better, more personal service. If you have any questions about the places you visit, there will always be a well-informed guide to give you the answer. In other companies, tour groups often have as many as fifty people per group, and this makes it difficult to have your questions answered.

So although our Tour of America may be a little more expensive than those offered by other companies, it is definitely worth the extra cost. Please let me know if you have any other questions, and I hope to see you soon on the best Tour of America.

Sincerely,
Thomas Adams
Sunshine Tours of America



Answer see page 112

____ 1. Why was this letter written?

A. This letter was written to describe five cities in America and say where they are.

B. This letter was written to complain about the Tour of America.

C. This letter was written to say why the Tour of America is better than other tours.

D. This letter was written to purchase some tickets to the Tour of America.

____ 2. Based on the information given in the letter, who are Mr. And Mrs. Lee?

A. They are people who are interested in the Tour of America.

B. They are people who have already gone on the Tour of America.

C. They are people who want to learn more about the city of Chicago.

D. They are tour guides who enjoy traveling in the United States.



Answer see page 113

____ 3. In which city will tourists spend four days shopping, going to museums and sightseeing around town?

A. San Francisco

B. New Orleans

C. New York

D. Chicago

____ 4. What are two advantages of the Tour of America as compared to the tours offered by other companies?

A. The Tour of America goes to more cities and costs less money.

B. The Tour of America has fewer tourists and goes to fewer cities.

C. The Tour of America goes to more cities and has fewer tourists.

D. The Tour of America costs less money but goes to more cities.



Answer see page 114

____ 5. According to the letter, what is the advantage of having fewer people in each group?

A. With fewer people the group can travel faster and have more fun.

B. With fewer people it is easier to ask the tour guides questions.

C. With fewer people it will be more difficult to get lost.

D. With fewer people the tour will cost less money per person.



Answer see page 114

## 7

Computers, televisions, airplanes, and automobiles are all examples of technology that have been developed within the last one hundred years. There is an ongoing argument that many people have about technology and its benefits to society. Most people agree that these machines help us to live easier and more convenient lives. Computers help us do our work faster, televisions can keep us informed, and airplanes and automobiles help us go from one place to another quickly. These are just a few of the advantages of modern technology.

Yet along with these obvious advantages, there are also some disadvantages to consider. Computers are expensive to operate and require that a person spend a lot of time learning how to use them. Sometimes computers can make mistakes and then waste a lot



Answer see page 115

of a person's time. And although televisions are great for getting information out to the public, many people waste too much time watching worthless, meaningless shows. Airplanes and automobiles help people travel faster, but they also cause accidents that kill many people every day.

As is often the case, there are two sides to this argument about technology. On the one hand, technology can make people's lives more efficient and convenient. But on the other hand, technology can also create new problems for people. Both sides of this argument are valid, and it's up to each individual to decide what role technology will play in their own life... and if it's worth it.



Answer see page 115

____ 1. Apart from those listed above, what are some other examples of technology?

A. Books and magazines.

B. Hamburgers and pizza.

C. Plants and animals.

D. Telephones and busses.

____ 2. Which of the following is an example of how technology can be beneficial to people?

A. Airplanes that crash and kill many people.

B. People who waste their time watching television every day.

C. Computers that help people do their work faster and easier.

D. Computers that are used incorrectly and cause people to redo their work.



Answer see page 116

____ 3. Which of the following is an example of how technology is not beneficial to people?

A. Airplanes and automobiles that let people travel easier.

B. Computers that help people do their work faster.

C. Televisions that people waste time watching.

D. Telephones that allow people to communicate easily.

____ 4. Which of the following best describes the opinion of this article?

A. Technology always helps people to live happier, easier and better lives and doesn't really have any disadvantages.

B. Technology causes more problems than it fixes and the world would be a much better place if there was no technology.



Answer see page 116

C. Technology can be both helpful and harmful. People need to decide for themselves how much technology they want in their lives.

D. Technology in the past was always very helpful but newer technology is increasingly problematic and troublesome.

____ 5. Which of the following is the best title for this essay?

A. A short history of the development of modern technology.

B. The many reasons why technology is one of mankind's greatest pursuits.

C. A discussion of the various advantages and disadvantages of technology in our world.

D. A look into the many problems that modern technology has created for modern humans.



Answer see page 117

## Note 這句英文，改變你的人生

- Public before private and country before family.
（先公而後私，先國而後家。）

- Be swift to hear slow to speak.
（敏捷的聽，緩慢的說。）

- The voice of the people is the voice of God.
（人民的聲音就是上帝的聲音。）

- Character is destiny.
（個性造就了命運。）

Chapter

# Answers and Analyses

# 解答 & 解析

## Part 1 Vocabulary Selection

# 第一部分

# 詞彙和結構

幾乎所有英語考試都會考詞彙和結構這類的單選試題。本題型主要是在測驗你對英語單字定義的熟悉程度。其他類考題則在測驗你對英語文法與閱讀的理解，因此應付這部分的試題，你應該先釐清每個單字的意義。

針對這個測驗，最好的準備方式就是盡可能的背誦許多英文單字。但是，不要灰心，這並不像聽起來那樣困難。熟記英文單字最好的方法就是每天學習幾個新單字，並持之以恆不斷地複習，直到你真正記住為止。除了熟知每個字的意義之外，你也應該練習用這些單字來造句。事實上，自己造出屬於自己的句子，也是記憶單字意義的好方法之一。

在這裡提供你一些值得記住的秘訣，對這部分測驗的答題會大有幫助：

在做選擇之前，先將所有的答案選項看過一遍：每次都會有四個選擇，有時候這些選項看起來似乎都是正確的，但總是有一些小問題，這些選項正是誤導應試者的障眼法！所以，請小心，將所有選項看過一遍之後，再選出一個最正確的答案。

第一題總是最簡單的，之後的問題會漸漸地增加困難度：英語考試當然不會只考一些大家都會的題目，在測驗中總會穿插一些非常困難的問題。你不必因此而擔心，當你讀到一個你不懂的答案，先從四個選項中刪掉你確定有錯的答案，藉由刪除一個到兩個不正確的答案，你找到正確答案的機率就會提高。

在後面的附錄部分有五十個例句。在你讀完這個部分後，你應該利用這些例句來幫助自己更了解這些單字，並有效記憶這些字彙，更應該了解他們在句子中的使用方法。

B 1. 只因為他的車______，所以他贏得比賽。

A. 吃素 B. 比較快 C. 慢下來 D. 比較慢

C 2. 如果老師讓我們在學校______這個作業，那我們就可以快一點完成。

A. 玩 B. 拿 C. 做 D. 帶

D 3. 當喬發現他的太太不在廚房的時候，他就走到______去找她。

A. 燈 B. 珠寶商 C. 嬸嬸 D. 臥室

C 4. 我們要求其他的學生______我們的團隊，這樣我們就會有更多人也能更迅速地工作。

A. 跳 B. 拜託 C. 加入 D. 借用

B 5. 他沒看到樹上的猴子，因為它在他頭的正______。

A. 附近 B. 上方 C. 在 D. 四周

B 6. 到這條河對岸唯一的方法，就是走過位於路底的那座______。

A. 建築物 B. 橋 C. 麵包店 D. 烤肉

C 7. 這位醫生立刻______幫助傷者。

A. 複習 B. 要求 C. 趕去 D. 拯救

A 8. 他已經工作十一個月，都沒有______，我想，他應該請幾天假。

A. 假期 B. 流浪的 C. 預防接種 D. 空

D 9. 我們花了兩個小時，找他掉在車子椅座______的車鑰匙。

A. 四周 B. 裡面 C. 附近 D. 下面

A 10. ______每天讀書，你才能在學校課業上有所成就。

A. 只有 B. 也 C. 當 D. 大約在

C 11. 他的電腦停止運轉，只因為它的______沒有任何電力了。

A. 步兵營 B. 被徵召者 C. 電池 D. 連接

A 12. 他的______狗跟著他到處走。

A. 忠實的 B. 移開的 C. 馬虎的 D. 維持的

B 13. ______他來自法國，但是他的英文和日文都非常流利。

A. 為了　B. 雖然　C. 之前　D. 代替

A 14. 這家銀行裝置了許多新的攝影機，以提高______程度。

A. 安全　B. 職業　C. 利息　D. 智慧

B 15. 我______你在批評這本書之前，先完全地了解書中所傳達的理念。

A. 娛樂　B. 建議　C. 批評　D. 證明

B 16. 如果你要上到那個村莊，那麼首先你必須先爬這座______。

A. 河流　B. 山　C. 平原　D. 三角洲

B 17. 老闆給他的祕書______指示，要求計畫在這個星期完成。

A. 不可避免的　B. 特定的
C. 被 的　D. 不高興的

C 18. 在我所有的______中，莎拉是唯一一個會忘記作業的人。

A. 學校　B. 校園　C. 同學　D. 圖書館

__B__ 19. 當這個男孩在跟他姊姊聊天的時候，他的三明治被鳥______了。

A. 偷走（過去分詞） B. 偷走（被 式）
C. 偷走（原形） D. 偷走（過去式）

__A__ 20. 這個政治家走進這個城鎮，要求人們______給他。

A. 投票 B. 測驗 C. 解釋 D. 管理

__C__ 21. 有一些來自美國的人初抵亞洲時，發現用______吃飯是很困難的。

A. 日曆 B. 優待券 C. 筷子 D. 卡片

__D__ 22. 我很抱歉，我今天晚上很忙，我們能改約______嗎？

A. 以後 B. 反省 C. 之後 D. 下午

__C__ 23. 這位醫生花了20分鐘的時間______這位生病的女孩之後，他給了她一些藥並告訴她要回家休息。

A. 解釋 B. 期待 C. 檢查 D. 引渡

__A__ 24. 哇，你聽到______了嗎？莎莉和傑夫要結婚了！

A. 消息 B. 景色 C. 審判 D. 測量

__A__ 25. ______健康問題產生的最好方式就是經常運 ，還有吃富含水果和蔬菜的健康飲食。

A. 預防　B. 獲得　C. 保存　D. 確定

__C__ 26. 因為這位歌手每次都表演得很好，大多數的歌迷覺得她表演水準相當______。

A. 徵兵　B. 相鄰的　C. 維持水平　D. 複雜的

__A__ 27. 這個電影明星相當注重______，所以他對新聞記者說話總是很小心。

A. 形象　B. 檢查　C. 魅力　D. 野心

__B__ 28. 我很想幫你，可是我就是______移 那些大石頭。

A. 不能的　B. 沒有能力的
C. 有問題的　D. 可預期的

__A__ 29. 因為我們這一隊發生太多延遲，______我們是否能準時完成。

A. 令人懷疑的　B. 啞然失聲的
C. 絕對的　D. 注定的

__C__ 30. 人們說，喝茶比喝______對身體健康有益。

A. 圓筒　B. 費多拉帽　C. 咖啡　D. 山丘

__B__ 31. 這個男孩的媽媽試著______他花太多時間玩電腦遊戲。

A. 支持　B. 阻止　C. 說服　D. 鼓勵

__A__ 32. 街上太多______，所以我聽不到你說什麼。

A. 噪音　B. 罪行　C. 人　D. 石頭

__B__ 33. 她現在餓到你可以聽到她的______一直發出聲音。

A. 肩膀　B. 肚子　C. 隔膜　D. 胸骨

__B__ 34. 她最______財產就是奶奶送給她的圖畫書。

A. 困難的　B. 珍貴的　C. 正確的　D. 全部的

__C__ 35. 如果我們那時都一起去看電影，______更有趣了。

A. 就會（未來式）　B. 就會（過去式）
C. 就會（過去完成式）　D. 就有（過去進行式）

__C__ 36. 我的朋友找到了一個在電腦店的工作，因為他想要學如何______損壞的電腦。

A. 表演　B. 減輕　C. 修理　D. 複雜

__B__ 37. 他唯一的壞______就是他抽菸。

A. 問題　B. 習慣　C. 才能　D. 期待

__B__ 38. 他的房子______很好，就在城市的中心。

A. 訊息　B. 位置　C. 嘗試　D. 書法

__B__ 39. 即使我們無法唸完這些書，______我們可以念其中的一部份。

A. 所有的　B. 至少　C. 永遠地　D. 如果全部

__A__ 40. 這個女孩跑進來，______告訴她的朋友她在街上撿到錢的事。

A. 興奮地　B. 期待地　C. 專業地　D. 令人厭煩地

__C__ 41. 人們期望，較好的______會使他們的生活更容易，且更具生產力。

A. 森林學　B. 生物學　C. 科技　D. 化學

B 42. 我們希望你不會遭遇太多______，就能找到你掉的皮夾。

A. 決定 B. 困難 C. 提及 D. 錯誤

D 43. 只有在經過一場漫長的討論之後，這對男女朋友才能______他們的問題。

A. 底線 B. 表演 C. 利用 D. 解決

A 44. 這個藝術家的______使他無法賣出他昂貴的畫作。

A. 貪婪 B. 才能 C. 表演 D. 有用

A 45. 這位警官認為這場火災是由一個危險的罪犯______引起的。

A. 蓄意 B. 完美地 C. 通常地 D. 期待地

A 46. 我的朋友比較喜歡看______，而沒有那麼喜歡報紙。

A. 雜誌 B. 微波 C. 使者 D. 惡棍

B 47. 群體決定他們應該等到明天再開會。

A. 決定（ 詞原形） B. 決定（被 式）
C. 決定（名詞） D. 決定（過去式）

__A__ 48. 老師們全部______練習說英文的最好方式是到國外唸書。

A. 同意（過去式）　B. 同意（名詞）
C. 同意（V+ing）　D. 宜人的

__D__ 49. 正當他們沿著街道______，就發現開始下雨了。

A. 走（原形）　B. 走（未來式）
C. 走（V+ing）　D. 走（過去進行式）

__A__ 50. 這個小男孩是以______每一個他說的故事而有名。

A. 誇大　B. 如果　C. 說服　D. 浪費

# Part 2 Cloze Section

## 第二部分

## 段落填空

大多數的英文測驗都有克漏字詞的部分。這與開頭的字彙選擇部分非常的相似。同樣的，其目的在於測驗你的英文字彙知識。

主要的不同是，克漏字部分是完整的段落，而不是單獨的句子。這一點可能會有所幫助，因為你可以利用上下文之間的線索來選擇正確的字。如果你了解每個段落的大概意思，那麼為每個空格找到一個正確的答案就比較容易。

這裡有幾個供記憶的秘訣，可以幫助你做克漏字的部分：

在選擇對的答案之前，記得將所有的選擇看過一遍：和第一部分一樣，有些選項總是幾可亂真，記得別被誤導，選出一個最正確的答案。

先將你確定有錯的答案刪除：如果你看不懂其中的選項，記得先將不正確的答案刪除，再作選擇。

注意字的結尾，尤其是動詞的部分：因為英文 詞會根據句子不同的時態而變化。如果你知道答案的正確時態，這就可以幫助你找到正確的答案。只要刪除時態錯誤的選項，再由剩下來的選項中選擇就可以。

## 1

Many young people enjoy ___1___ sports. Basketball is one sport very ___2___ with young people, ___3___ boys. Many boys play ___4___ of basketball while in high school, some even play for their school's basketball ___5___. Because they practice ___6___, some of them get ___7___ very good at basketball. Some of these basketball ___8___ even hope to play professionally someday. But it's very difficult to ___9___ a professional basketball player, and very few of those who try ever ___10___.

許多年輕人喜歡從事運動。籃球是在年輕人之間深受歡迎的一種運動，尤其是男孩們。在高中期間，許多男孩常常打籃球，有些人甚至成為籃球校隊的球員。因為他們常常練習，他們有些人變得很會打籃球。這些籃球隊員中有一些甚至希望有一天能成為職業選手。但是，要成為一個職業籃球運動員並不容易，而且只有少數的人得以成功。

B 1. A. player
B. playing
C. play
D. played

C 2. A. excited
B. famous
C. popular
D. fun

B 3. A. also
B. especially
C. without
D. for

C 4. A. lot
B. many
C. a lot
D. much

A 5. A. team
B. group
C. division
D. unit

B 6. A. quickly
B. often
C. usually
D. only

A 7. A. to be
B. are
C. be
D. is

C 8. A. play
B. player
C. players
D. playing

B 9. A. change
B. become
C. attest
D. decide

A 10. A. succeed
B. successful
C. success
D. succeeding

## 2

People ____1____ the world use many different methods to build houses. Those who live in areas with forests and many trees often build their homes out of wood, because it's most ____2____. People who live in areas where there are no trees must find ____3____ materials with which to build. For ____4____, people who live in desert areas often use rocks or clay to build houses, ____5____ those who live in jungle areas often use wood and leaves. People are very ____6____, and have used many other things to provide shelter. When wood, rocks and clay are not easily ____7____, then people use a ____8____ of other materials. People in cities use brick and ____9____ to make buildings, while the Inuit of the snowy arctic ____10____ use only snow!

世界各地的人使用許多不同的方法建造房屋。那些住在森林或是林木豐富的區域的人經常用木材建造他們的家，因為它是最容易取得的建材。住區沒有木材的人則必須找其他材料來蓋房子。例如，住在沙漠地區的人經常使用岩石或黏土來建造房屋，而那些住在叢林區域的人經常使用木材與樹葉。人類是很聰明的，懂得利用許多其他的東西來提供遮蔽處。當木頭、岩石及黏土都不易取得時，人們會利用一些其他的材料。在城市中的人用磚塊與鋼鐵來蓋建築物，而住在多雪的北極的愛斯基摩人只用雪來蓋房子！

C 1. A. about
B. above
C. around
D. along

B 2. A. destroyed
B. available
C. sympathetic
D. terrified

A 3. A. other
B. equal
C. uniform
D. certain

C 4. A. argument
B. sake
C. example
D. reasons

B 5. A. which
B. while
C. without
D. whence

C 6. A. resourceful
B. irritating
C. wise
D. expendable

C 7. A. forgotten
B. expensive
C. found
D. enjoyed

B 8. A. system
B. variety
C. class
D. tempest

B 9. A. fabric
B. steel
C. tempo
D. patent

C 10. A. dilemmas
B. experts
C. regions
D. attitudes

## 3

Sharks are ＿＿1＿＿ of the most ＿＿2＿＿ animals on the planet. For ＿＿3＿＿ as mankind has known about sharks, they ＿＿4＿＿ feared. But actually, sharks pose very little ＿＿5＿＿ to most people. Sharks usually stay away from humans, and ＿＿6＿＿ very rarely swim near beaches or other areas with many people. Many scientists ＿＿7＿＿ that when sharks do attack people, it's only because the sharks have ＿＿8＿＿ the person for another animal, like a seal. There have been many movies made ＿＿9＿＿ sharks, and most show sharks as being vicious and dangerous creatures. But in ＿＿10＿＿, sharks kill very few people, and overall mankind benefits from their presence in the oceans.

鯊魚是地球上最讓人害怕的動物之一。自從人們對鯊魚有了認識後，就已經害怕這種生物。但是實際上，鯊魚對多數人來說，威脅並不大。鯊魚通常不會出現在人類面前，而且只有少數時候會游近海灘或其他人多的地方。許多科學家相信，鯊魚會攻擊人類，是因為鯊魚把人誤認為其他動物，例如：海豹。有許多關於鯊魚的電影，常把鯊魚拍成惡毒且危險的生物。但是，在現實生活中，鯊魚殺害的人相當少，且整體而言，海中的鯊魚對人類還算是頗有貢獻。

D 1. A. many
B. some
C. especially
D. one

A 2. A. feared
B. helpless
C. expectant
D. alleged

B 3. A. as in
B. as long
C. as for
D. as if

B 4. A. been
B. have been
C. will be
D. was

A 5. A. threat
B. excuse
C. trouble
D. question

B 6. A. always
B. only
C. then
D. askew

C 7. A. research
B. experiment
C. believe
D. portray

A 8. A. mistaken
B. convinced
C. expected
D. attained

B 9. A. for
B. about
C. within
D. while

D 10. A. real
B. realistic
C. realism
D. reality

## 4

Do you believe ____1____ ghosts? Many people ____2____ that because science hasn;t proven that ghosts are real, then they cannot be real. These people say that because ____3____ are not any machines or scientific instruments that can help us find ghosts, then they must not be real. But other people have different ____4____. These people say that ____5____ science can;t prove ghosts are real, science ____6____ can-not prove ghosts are not real. So there really are two ____7____ to this argument. This is an issue that in the future may never ____8____. But what do you ____9____? Have you ____10____ seen a ghost?

你相信鬼嗎？很多人說因為科學還無法證明真的有鬼，所以鬼不可能是真的。這些人說，因為沒有任何機器或科學儀器可以幫助我們找出鬼，那鬼就一定不是真的。但是其他的人有不同的意見。這些人說，雖然科學不能證明鬼魂是真的，同樣的科學亦不能證明鬼魂不是真的。所以，這個討論有兩造的意見。這個議題可能在未來也沒辦法解決。那你有什麼看法呢？你曾經看過鬼嗎？

B 1. A. of
B. in
C. on
D. at

A 2. A. say
B. saying
C. said
D. says

C 3. A. this
B. those
C. there
D. then

A 4. A. opinions
B. requirements
C. uses
D. terms

D 5. A. already
B. always
C. altogether
D. although

A 6. A. also
B. and
C. but
D. for

B 7. A. people
B. sides
C. places
D. machines

B 8. A. will resolve
B. be resolved
C. resolving
D. have resolved

A 9. A. think
B. thought
C. thinking
D. will think

D 10. A. always
B. evenly
C. but
D. ever

## 5

Christopher Columbus is one of the most ___1___ explorers in Western history. He was the ___2___ European to sail to the Americas. However, he made many mistakes along the way. First of all, he ___3___ he had arrived in India when he had actually arrived in the central American ___4___. For this ___5___, he called the people of Central America "Indians". Also, he got lost ___6___ the times. Back in the 15th ___7___, sailors used the stars to steer their ships. Some sailors were very good at this, but Columbus was not. ___8___ one occasion, he used the stars to calculate that he ___9___ near a certain island in the Caribbean, when actually ___10___ was over two thousand kilometers away!

克利斯多夫· 哥倫布是西方歷史中最有名的探險家之一。他是第一位航行到美洲的歐洲人。然而，一路上他犯了許多錯誤。首先，他以為自己抵達了印度，而實際上他是抵達了中美洲地區。這也是為什麼，他把中美洲人稱為「印地安人」。還有，他總是搞錯方向。在十五世紀那時候，水手習慣依靠星星來決定船航行的方向。

有些水手非常善於此法，但是哥倫布不是這種人。有一次，他利用星星計算出他正在某加勒比海小島附近，但實際上，他離那裡有兩千多公里遠！

__B__ 1. A. perfect
B. famous
C. useful
D. efficient

__A__ 2. A. first
B. begin
C. former
D. start

__C__ 3. A. think
B. thinking
C. thought
D. will think

__D__ 4. A. place
B. country
C. citizen
D. region

__A__ 5. A. reason
B. motive
C. alibi
D. excuse

__C__ 6. A. one
B. many
C. all
D. each

__B__ 7. A. time
B. century
C. week
D. hour

__B__ 8. A. At
B. On
C. Of
D. Or

__C__ 9. A. were
B. is
C. was
D. are

__D__ 10. A. she
B. they
C. we
D. he

## Part 3 Reading Comprehension Section

## 第三部分

# 閱讀理解

這是所有英文閱讀測驗中涵蓋範圍最廣的部分，因為這測驗的目的在測試你對文法、字彙的認識，以及你對英語文章整體的意思與細節部分掌握多少。

這裡有一些秘訣能幫助你回答閱讀理解部分的問題：

在開始讀文章之前，先把題目與選項瀏覽過一遍：這個技巧非常重要；在你還不知道文章主題之前，先將題目看一遍，這樣你才可以在讀文章的同時抓住題目要問的細節。記住：一定要先看題目！

在每個問題中找出關鍵字：有時候，題目包含不同的片語，句子就會很長。如果你能辨識出題目中重要的片語，你找到正確答案的機會就大大地增加。

注意問題使用的替代字：有時候，題目會出現一些文章單字的同義字；例如：題目可能會問在文章中某事如何「改善」了，但是在文章中卻有可能是用「變得更好」來描述。

## 1

今年夏天我有一個很愉快的假期。在六月，就在我們學校開始放暑假的時候，我和家人到紐柏理埠去看奶奶和爺爺。紐柏理埠是一個靠海的小鎮。爺爺、奶奶在那裡已經住了好多年，但是那邊離我的家很遠，所以，我們一年只能來這裡幾次。

我們和爺爺、奶奶度過了一段很美好的時光。有一天，我們去海灘玩，我們撿了許多貝殼，還很開心地放了風箏。第二天，爺爺帶哥哥跟我乘他的帆船出去航海。哇！航海真有趣，而爺爺也是個很棒的水手。第三天，我們到附近的一個湖邊釣魚。我哥哥抓到兩條大魚，但是我一條也沒釣到。我們把魚帶回家，奶奶煮了魚當晚餐。真的好好吃！

當我們從紐柏理埠回來之後，我哥哥和我參加了一個夏令營。我們在那裡待了五天。我們每天都做了許多有趣的事情。我們玩遊戲、游泳、説故事、在森林中散步；晚上我們總是有很大的營火。對我來説，這是個非常有趣的暑假！我希望下一個假期可以跟這個假期一樣好玩！

B 1. 哪一個標題最適合這個女孩的文章?

A. 為什麼我的爺爺、奶奶住在紐柏理埠?

B. 我在暑假做了什麼事?

C. 我為什麼那麼喜歡我哥哥?

D. 我在暑假見到了哪些人?

A 2. 下列哪一個是她在暑假中所有事情的正確發生順序?

A. 首先她到紐柏理埠，然後去航海，之後再去夏令營。

B. 首先她去夏令營，然後去航海，之後再去看她的爺爺、奶奶。

C. 首先她去釣魚，然後去航海，之後再去紐柏理埠。

D. 首先她去紐柏理埠，然後去夏令營，之後再去航海。

C 3. 下列何者不是她在夏令營裡做的事情?

A. 游泳。

B. 散步。

C. 騎腳踏車。

D. 說故事。

B 4. 這個女孩說她在哪裡放了風箏?

A. 她在夏令營裡放了風箏。

B. 她在海灘上放了風箏。

C. 她在夏令營裡和海灘上放了風箏。

D. 她並沒有放風箏。

## 2

親愛的李昆，

你還記得我嗎？我是你的老朋友，詹姆士· 李。我已經很長一段時間沒有寫信給你了，所以，我想跟你談一下我的近況。過去的兩年中，我住在加拿大的溫哥華。我在那的第一年，是在溫哥華大學修習英語與英國文學。這是一所很好的學校，在那裡唸書讓我的英文進步很多。當我剛到加拿大的時候，我覺得用英文與人溝通很困難，但是現在它已經不是問題了。

最近，我在溫哥華鬧區的一家義大利餐廳工作。我的工作是負責煮湯和沙拉。這是一個有趣的工作，因為我可以學做許多義大利料理，而且和我一起工作的人都對我很好。我一個星期只工作四天，所以，我有足夠的時間去觀光，探索溫哥華這個城市。

溫哥華是加拿大西岸的一座大城市。這真是個很漂亮的城市，有許多公園、山岳，甚至還有一個海灘！在靠近溫哥華的海邊有許多小島，我有去過其中的幾個，它們充滿自然的美麗。大體而言，溫哥華是個很棒的地方，而我很高興我決定到這裡來。如果你想要來加拿大，讓我知道，因為我會很高興看到你來。

你的朋友，<br>詹姆士· 李

__A__ 1. 詹姆士· 李和李昆是誰?

A. 他們是很久以前的朋友。

B. 他們是同一所學校的學生。

C. 他們在同一家餐廳工作。

D. 他們是彼此不認識的人。

__B__ 2. 根據這封信，詹姆士· 李上一次寫信給李昆是什麼時候?

A. 幾天前。

B. 很久以前。

C. 從來沒寫過。

D. 上個星期。

__B__ 3. 詹姆士· 李在溫哥華住多久了?

A. 一年。

B. 兩年。

C. 三年。

D. 四年。

__D__ 4. 關於他剛抵達加拿大的時候，詹姆士說了些什麼?

A. 他說他的英文說得很好。

B. 他說他不說英文。

C. 他說他只說義大利文。

D. 他說用英文溝通很困難。

B 5. 詹姆士· 李如何改善他的英語能力?

A. 他練習聽英語電視節目。

B. 他在大學裡讀英語與英國文學。

C. 他在許多說英語的餐廳裡工作。

D. 他的英文一直都很好，不需要進步。

D 6. 詹姆士喜歡他的工作嗎? 為什麼喜歡或者為什麼不喜歡?

A. 他不喜歡他的工作，因為工作很難而且他得每天工作。

B. 他喜歡他的工作，因為他可以免費吃許多義大利食物。

C. 他不喜歡他的工作，因為跟他一起工作的人不是好人。

D. 他喜歡他的工作，因為他可以學做義大利料理。

D 7. 在信的最後，詹姆士說了什麼?

A. 他說他很後悔搬到溫哥華，因為它不是一個好城市，而且他必須很辛苦地工作。

B. 他說雖然溫哥華是一座很好的城市，但是他要搬到美國唸書。

C. 他說溫哥華之前是座很好的城市，但是現在人太多，他想搬到其他的地方去。

D. 他說他很高興自己住在溫哥華，如果他的朋友來拜訪他，他會很高興。

## 3

這個星期六下午，從一點到晚上十點，在希斯巴羅鬧區帕克街上的希斯巴羅小學裡將會舉辦嘉年華園遊會。這個園遊會將提供許多遊戲、多樣豐富食物、一場音樂表演，還有許多參與者可以贏走的獎品。

那裡還會有大型的戶外烤肉，由晚上六點開始直到食物吃完為止！漢堡、熱狗、沙拉還有飲料都會免費提供給 買嘉年華園遊會入場券的人。艾維斯搖滾樂團也會有一場音樂表演，表演由八點開始直到嘉年華會結束。這場表演也是免費給所有購買園遊會入場券的人聆賞。

嘉年華園遊會入場券的票價，大人是五元，小孩是三元。園遊會所有的收入將捐給希斯巴羅小學的圖書館，以供採購新書及電腦。所以，我們希望這個星期六你們大家都能來，在嘉年華園遊會中開心的玩，同時也支持希斯巴羅小學的圖書館。所以咱們就到那裡見囉！

<u>D</u> 1. 下列哪一個標題最適合這篇文章?

A. 艾維斯搖滾樂團錄製了一張新專輯。

B. 烤肉會有漢堡、熱狗和沙拉。

C. 希斯巴羅小學有很有趣的學生。

D. 在希斯巴羅小學的嘉年華園遊會。

<u>B</u> 2. 下列關於嘉年華園遊會的敘述哪一個正確?

A. 會有音樂、遊戲，但是不會有任何食物。

B. 會有音樂、遊戲還有一個烤肉會。

C. 只有食物和遊戲，沒有任何音樂。

D. 會有許多書和電腦可供使用。

<u>A</u> 3. 下列關於嘉年華園遊會的敘述哪一個正確?

A. 如果你買一張園遊會的票，你就可以免費吃烤肉並參加艾維斯搖滾樂團的演唱會。

B. 如果你買一張園遊會的票，你要另外買票才能參加烤肉以及艾維斯搖滾樂團的表演。

C. 如果你買一張烤肉會的票，那你也可以免費去參加園遊會以及艾維斯搖滾樂團的音樂會。

D. 如果買了艾維斯搖滾樂團的票，那你可以免費參加圓遊會。

__B__ 4. 希斯巴羅小學為什麼舉辦嘉年華園遊會?

A. 他們要學生學習搖滾樂的知識。

B. 他們會用賣票得來的錢為圖書館添購東西。

C. 他們喜歡做有趣的事情，例如：舉行烤肉會以及玩遊戲。

D. 他們需要賣很多票才能負擔烤肉的成本。

親愛的湯瑪士先生，

你好嗎？我過得不是很順利。你記不記得你借給我的相機？呃，很抱歉要這麼説，因為發生了一些小問題，所以我把它弄丟了。當然，我會賠錢讓你可以買一個新的相機，但首先讓我告訴你事情的始末。

上個星期五，就在你借給我相機的那一天，我到海灘上去晃晃。那天雖然有一點風，但是天氣很好。我邊往海邊走邊照相，然後我看到一個男人坐在一條小船上。這個男人跟我聊天，並且問我想不想坐船出海一趟。所以，我就跟他坐船兜風去。

大約過了二十分鐘，太陽開始往下沈。天空變成橘色與紅色，看起來非常美麗。所以我開始對著夕陽照相，突然間一個大浪打過來，打中了我們的小船！相機從我手上被打進海裡，它像一顆石頭般的沈入水中。我覺得好難過，因為當時我一點兒辦法也沒有！

所以，真的很對不起把你的相機弄丟。我希望你能了解，這是一件意外。不過不管如何，請務必告知我買一台新相機的價格，我會馬上把錢還你。希望你這次可以原諒我！

萬分地抱歉，

傑夫· 戴維斯

B 1. 傑夫· 戴維斯為什麼要寫這封信?

A. 他因為要向湯瑪士先生借照相機，所以寫了這封信。

B. 他寫這封信告訴湯瑪士先生，他把向他借的照相機弄丟了。

C. 他因為湯瑪士先生要向他借照相機，所以寫了這封信。

D. 他因為要找到湯瑪士先生的照相機，所以寫這封信。

C 2. 那個形容最適合描述傑夫· 戴維斯在信中的感覺和語氣?

A. 生氣和難過。

B. 有趣和高興。

C. 遺憾和抱歉。

D. 無理和苛求。

D 3. 下列哪個是信中事件發生的正確順序?

A. 傑夫借了照相機，後來弄丟了，之後他搭船出遊。

B. 傑夫搭船出遊，後來借了照相機，之後他把它弄丟了。

C. 傑夫弄丟了照相機，後來他去了海灘，再搭船出遊。

D. 傑夫借了照相機，再搭船出遊，之後他把照相機弄丟了。

B 4. 傑夫說他要怎麼做?

A. 他說他以後不會再向湯瑪士先生借照相機。

B. 他說他會給湯瑪士先生錢買新的照相機。

C. 他說他會把照相機借給湯瑪士先生。

D. 他說湯瑪士先生不應該那麼不注意他的照相機。

## 5

大多數的人知道，美國人愛車。當然，情況並不是從以前就是這樣的。一直到1950年代，美國人主要是依靠火車和公車作為交通工具。這是因為當時一般的美國人認為買車、維護及修理的費用太昂貴了。但是，在1950年代一切都改變了，原因有好幾個。

第二次世界大戰在1945年結束，美國開始了一段工業發展的時期。許多戰爭中退下來的工廠與機械，都被改裝來創造新的產品。在戰爭期間製造武器的工程師與工廠工人，轉而開始為一般大眾製造產品。他們開始製造的產品中有一項就是汽車，而因為他們的努力，汽車才比以前更便宜，品質也比較好。

不久後，更多美國人開始 買這些比較便宜的汽車，而這引起了政府的注意。政府知道此後國家需要更多、更好的馬路與公路。因此，在1950年代中的許多年，政府將許多稅款用在建造新的公路上，以連接所有的州；由東到西，由北到南。而美國人一看到這些新的公路，他們作何反應呢？他們就買更多的車囉！

現在，過了五十多年後，美國人開始體認到路上太多汽車可能會造成問題。在美國大多數的城市中，路上的汽車都太多，造成交通緩慢。汽車還造成空氣污染，這讓人們開始擔心種種對環境的影響。因為這些原因，許多美國人選擇不開車。那他們改搭什麼呢？他們又回到搭乘火車和公車的時代！

__C__ 1. 以下哪個標題最適合這篇文章?

A. 火車和公車比汽車好。

B. 第二次世界大戰與美國的馬路。

C. 汽車在美國的簡短歷史。

D. 汽車對環境有害。

__A__ 2. 1950年代以前，為什麼只有少數美國人有車?

A. 因為車子很昂貴，維修費也高。

B. 因為汽車產生太多的空氣污染。

C. 因為製造汽車的工廠很忙。

D. 因為大多數的美國人不會開車。

__B__ 3. 第二次世界大戰結束如何影響美國的汽車製造?

A. 當戰爭結束後，更多人有時間學習如何製造自己的汽車。

B. 大戰後，許多工廠與機器被改裝生產新產品，例如汽車。

C. 當戰爭結束後，沒有人還想要製造汽車，所以他們繼續製造武器。

D. 戰爭的結束使人們發覺，機械與科技並沒有幫助。

__C__ 4. 當政府發現許多美國人在買車時，它採取什麼樣的措施?

A. 政府開始想辦法解決城市的交通以及環境污染的問題。

B. 政府決定汽車實在是太昂貴，所以他們要汽車公司將車便宜點賣。

C. 政府開始建造更多新的道路，來連接這個國家的所有部分。

D. 政府開始讓人們免費搭公車與火車。

__B__ 5. 美國的汽車過多會有哪一些問題?

A. 它們產生失業與貧窮。

B. 它們產生污染和交通問題。

C. 它們對工廠造成問題。

D. 它們創造出更多且更好的馬路。

__A__ 6. 根據這篇文章，因為太多汽車所造成的問題，讓一些美國人開始做什麼?

A. 他們重新開始將公車與火車當作代步工具。

B. 他們要求政府不要再建造新的馬路。

C. 他們賣了汽車，而購買腳踏車。

D. 他們學習如何自己修理汽車。

親愛的李先生與李太太，

感謝你們對美國旅遊所提供的套裝行程表示興趣。在此，我希望多給你們一些相關的旅遊資訊，讓你們了解本公司提供的行程比其他公司好的原因。

首先，本公司會帶你們到五個美國的城市，而其他的旅行團大部分都只玩二、三個城市而已。我們的旅程從加州舊金山開始，然後去德州的奧斯丁。在那裡停留兩天之後，我們會往南到路易斯安納州南方的紐奧良。離開路易斯安納州，我們會北上到個很棒的城市──紐約。在這裡，你們可以花四天的時間購物、參觀博物館，以及在城裡觀光。在最後，我們會到中西部的城市──芝加哥，也就是「風城」。如果你們選擇的是別家旅行社，他們只會安排你們到其中二、三個地方而已！

本行程的第二個優點是旅行團的大小。我們將旅行團的大小限制在十五個人以內。為什麼呢？因為這樣，我們的導遊可以給你們更好、更個人化的服務。如果你們對造訪的地方有任何的問題，隨時隨地都會有位知識豐富的導遊給您答案。其他公司的旅遊團，一個團經常多達五十個人，這樣你們有任何問題恐怕都很難被照顧到。

所以，雖然我們美國旅遊的價格可能比起其他公司來得貴一些，但這絕對是值回票價的。如果你們有任何問題，請務必聯絡我。希望很快能見到你們來參加美國最好的旅遊團。

衷心的祝福您，
湯瑪士・亞當斯
美國陽光旅遊



__C__ 1. **這封信的目的是什麼?**

A. 這封信形容美國的五個都市，並說明它們的地理位置。

B. 這封信抱怨美國的旅遊行程。

C. 這封信說明為什麼美國旅遊比其他的旅遊行程來得好。

D. 這封信是用來替美國旅遊買某些票券的。

__A__ 2. **根據信中所給的資料，李先生與李太太是誰?**

A. 他們是對美國旅遊有興趣的人。

B. 他們是已經隨著美國旅遊行程旅行的人。

C. 他們是想要多了解芝加哥這個城市的人。

D. 他們是喜歡在美國旅行的導遊。

__C__ 3. 在那個城市，遊客會花四天的時間在「購物、參觀博物館與城市內的觀光活動」?

A. 舊金山。

B. 紐奧良。

C. 紐約。

D. 芝加哥。

__C__ 4. 與其他公司所提供的旅遊行程相比，美國旅遊有哪兩項優點?

A. 美國旅遊遊覽的城市較多且費用較低。

B. 美國旅遊的團員較少且去較少城市。

C. 美國旅遊遊覽的城市較多且團員較少。

D. 美國旅遊所需的費用較低但去的城市較多。

__B__ 5. 根據這封信，一團中的團員較少有什麼好處?

A. 團員較少，團體行動可以迅速些且較有趣。

B. 團員較少，要問導遊問題比較容易。

C. 團員較少，團員比較不容易走失。

D. 團員較少，每個團員花的錢比較少。

## 7

電腦、電視、飛機，以及汽車都是在近一百年內誕生的科技產物。長久以來，許多人對科技以及它給社會所帶來的好處一直爭論不休。許多人同意這些機械幫助我們，使生活更容易、更方便。電腦幫助我們加快工作的速度；電視使我們得知很多事情，而飛機和汽車讓我們能更快速地由一個地方移 到另一個地方。這些只是現代科技所帶來的少數好處。

但是，跟隨著這些明顯的好處，也有一些壞處要考慮。電腦操作起來很昂貴，而且需要一個人花許多時間學習如何使用。有時候電腦也會出錯，最後浪費了使用者很多的時間。還有，雖然電視是一個將資訊公開的很好方式，但是很多人浪費太多時間，觀看一些無價值、無意義的節目。飛機和汽車幫助人們能更快速地旅行，同樣地每天也發生造成許多人死亡的意外。

正如常例，這個針對科技的爭論也有兩方的意見。一方面，科技使人們的生活更有效率、更便利。但另一方面，科技也能為人們創造新的問題。爭論的兩方都是有根據的，而科技在生活中扮演什麼樣的角色，是否值得每個人去克服它帶來的問題……等，都是人人意見不同的。

D 1. 除了上列的例子，還有哪些其他的科技發展例子呢?

A. 書與雜誌。

B. 漢堡和披薩。

C. 植物與動物。

D. 電話和公共汽車。

C 2. 以下哪一個是科技對人們有利的例子?

A. 飛機墜機，許多人因此死亡。

B. 每天浪費時間在看電視的人。

C. 電腦幫助人能更快速且容易的做好他們的工作。

D. 不正確的使用電腦，使得人們必須重新把事情做一遍。

C 3. 下例哪一個是科技對人們有害的例子?

A. 使人們旅行起來更容易的飛機與汽車。

B. 使人們能更迅速地處理工作的電腦。

C. 讓人浪費時間的電視。

D. 讓人們溝通更容易的電話。

C 4. 下列哪個句子最適合描述這篇文章中的意見?

A. 科技總是幫助人們生活得更快樂、更容易、更好，而沒有真正的壞處。

B. 科技造成的問題比它解決的還多。如果這個世界上沒有科技會更好。

C. 科技可以幫助人，也可以傷害人。人們需要考慮自己的生活中科技要佔多大的地位。

D. 過去的科技總是非常有用，但是較新的科技逐漸地產生問題，也更麻煩。

C 5. 下列哪一個選項最適合作為這篇文章的標題?

A. 現代科技發展的簡短歷史。

B. 科技為什麼是人類最重要的追求目標之一。

C. 論科技帶給世界的好處與壞處。

D. 科技為現代人們所造成的許多問題的探討。

## Note 這句英文，改變你的人生

- Beware of a silent dog and still water.
  （小心悶不吭聲的狗和靜止的水。）

- He who begins many things finishes but few.
  （多頭馬車，一事無成。）

- When you play, play hard. When you work, don't play at all.
  （盡情玩樂，努力工作。）

Chapter

# All Three Sections

## 重點總整理

# Vocabulary Selection

## 1. faster 比較快

The cat can run much faster than the mouse.
貓跑得比老鼠快。

## 2. work 做（工作）

That homework was difficult. I had to work on it for four hours before I finished.
這個作業很難，我花了四個小時才完成。

## 3. bedroom 臥室

My sister is very lazy, so she sometimes spends all day in her bedroom.
我的妹妹很懶惰，有時候她一整天都待在臥室裡。

## 4. join 加入

The best baseball player always wants to join the best team.
最好的棒球選手當然希望加入最好的棒球隊。

## 5. above 上方

The birds were flying high above us.
這群鳥高高地從我們的上頭飛過。

### 6. bridge 橋

This bridge goes to the other side of the river.
這座橋穿越了這條河流到了對岸。

### 7. rushed 趕去

The people rushed to get to the movie theater before the movie started.
大家匆忙地趕到電影院，就怕趕不上電影開始。

### 8. vacation 假期

This summer we will go on vacation to Malaysia.
這個夏天我們會到馬來西亞去度假。

### 9. under 下面

We couldn't find the key because someone put it under the carpet.
我們找不到鑰匙，因為有人把它放在地毯下。

### 10. only if 唯有

Only if you pay the money can I let you use the video game.
唯有付錢，我才會讓你玩這個電動遊戲。

## 11. batteries 電池

His camera uses batteries very fast. He has to buy new batteries almost every day.

他的照相機耗電量很大，他幾乎每天都要買新電池。

## 12. faithful 忠實的

His faithful friend always helps him when he has a problem.

當他有困難的時候，他忠實的朋友總是會幫助他。

## 13. although 雖然

Although she doesn't like spicy food, she will eat it sometimes.

雖然她不喜歡吃辣，但她有時候還是會吃一點。

## 14. security 安全

The woman likes having a big dog because it gives her more security.

這個女人喜歡養大狗，因為大狗帶給她更多的安全感。

## 15. suggest 建議

I suggest you bring an umbrella because I think it will rain soon.

我建議你帶把傘出門，因為我覺得待會兒會下雨。

**16. mountain 山**

A mountain is bigger and taller than a hill.
山比丘陵高大。

**17. specific 確切的**

It will be difficult to find his house unless he gives you specific instructions.
除非他給你確切的指示，不然很難找到他的房子。

**18. classmates 同學**

Most of my classmates are the same age as me.
我大部分的同學年紀都跟我一樣大。

**19. was stolen 被偷**

The diamond was stolen by thieves.
鑽石被小偷偷走了。

**20. vote 投票**

He will be elected president if more than 50 percent of the people vote for him.
如果百分之五十以上的投票人將票投給他，他就會當選主席。

04

## 21. chopsticks 筷子

Chopsticks were invented by the Chinese many years ago.
筷子是許多年以前，由中國人發明的。

## 22. afternoon 下午

The time of day called "afternoon" is between noon and evening.
一天中稱作「下午」的時段是介於正午與晚上之間。

## 23. examining 檢查

The pilot is examining the airplane to make sure it's safe to fly.
這個飛行員檢查飛機，確保飛行的安全沒有問題。

## 24. news 消息

The good news is we found your wallet, the bad news is all of your money is missing.
好消息是，我們找到了你的錢包；壞消息是，你的錢都不見了。

## 25. prevent 預防

It is better to prevent health problems than cure them after they've started.
預防建康方面的毛病勝於事後治療。

### 26. consistent 一致的

His test scores are very consistent. He scores an 89 or a 90 on every test.

他的測驗成績總是相當一致。他每次考試不是考89分就是90分。

### 27. image 形象

The policeman's image worsened after the newspaper reported he took money from a criminal.

報紙報導出這個警員收受犯人的賄款後，他的形象就更差了。

### 28. incapable 不能的

If you are incapable of doing something, then there is no way for you to do it.

如果你不能做某件事，是指你沒有能力去做這件事。

### 29. doubtful 令人懷疑的

Unless you can work faster, it's doubtful you'll be able to finish on time.

除非你能做快一點，否則你不太可能準時完工。

### 30. coffee 咖啡

Coffee is a drink that is very popular all over the world.

咖啡是風靡全世界的飲品。

05

## 31. discourage 阻止

The doctor always discourages his patients and friends from drinking too much alcohol and smoking cigarettes.

醫生總是不鼓勵患者及朋友飲酒過量及吸煙。

## 32. noise 噪音

The children playing in the playroom are making a lot of noise.

在遊戲室裡玩的孩子們，正製造出大量的噪音。

## 33. stomach 胃

After you chew and swallow food, it goes into your stomach.

食物在經過人的咀嚼與吞嚥後，就進入胃中。

## 34. precious 珍貴的

Gold and silver are precious metals, but steel is not.

金和銀是珍貴的金屬，但鋼則不是。

## 35. would have been 應該會

It would have been better if you had studied more before taking the exam.

要是你當初在考試前多唸點書，情況應該會比較好。

## 36. repair 修理

After I broke my friend's computer, I gave him some money to repair it.
把朋友的電腦弄壞後，我就給了他一些修理費。

## 37. habit 習慣

A habit is something that you do often, even without intending to do it.
習慣是你經常做出來的舉動，甚至是無意識的。

## 38. location 位置

The soldiers used a compass to find the location of the airport.
士兵利用指南針找到了機場的方位。

## 39. at least 至少

Even if you can't see all the cities in Canada, at least you'll see a few of them.
即使你不能參觀加拿大的所有城市，至少你還可以參觀幾個。

## 40. excitedly 興奮地

The boy ran to his parents and excitedly told them about finding a small dog on the street.
男孩跑向他的父母親，並興奮地告訴他們，他在街上找到了一隻小狗。

## 41. technology 科技

The rich countries usually have much better technology than the poor ones.
富有國家的科技通常比貧窮國家的要好得多。

## 42. difficulties 困難

Because he couldn't speak English, he had difficulties talking to the Americans.
因為他不會說英語，所以跟美國人交談會有困難。

## 43. resolve 解決

The two countries are trying to resolve their problems.
這兩個國家正試著解決他們的問題。

## 44. greed 貪心

That man's greed is really too much, he never gives anything to anyone.
這個人真是貪婪的過分；他從來不願意分享東西給其他人。

## 45. deliberately 故意地

It wasn't an accident that he took your pencil case, he did it deliberately.
他不是不小心拿錯你的鉛筆盒，他是故意的。

### 46. magazines 雜誌

There are many magazines for sale that will help you study English.
坊間販售多種可以幫助你學習英語的雜誌。

### 47. was decided 被決定

It was decided by the group that they would first go to dinner and then see a movie.
先吃晚餐再去看電影，是多數人決定的結果。

### 48. agreed 同意

They talked about the problem for two hours before they agreed on how they would resolve it.
他們花了二小時討論這個問題，最後才達成如何解決的共識。

### 49. were walking 走

The boy and girl were walking in the woods when they saw the wolf.
當這個男孩和女孩看到這頭狼時，他們正走在森林裡。

### 50. exaggerating 吹牛

The old man was only exaggerating when he said the fish he caught was 3 meters long.
這個老人說他抓到的魚有三公尺長的時候，只是在吹牛。

# Cloze Section

07

Many young people enjoy playing sports. Basketball is one sport very famous with young people, especially boys. Many boys play a lot of basketball while in high school, some even play for their school's basketball team. Because they practice often, some of them get to be very good at basketball. Some of these basketball players even hope to play professionally someday. But it's very difficult to become a professional basketball player, and very few of those who try ever succeed.



Translation see page 88

People around the world use many different methods to build houses. Those who live in areas with forests and many trees often build their homes out of wood, because it's most available. People who live in areas where there are no trees must find other materials with which to build. For example, people who live in desert areas often use rocks or clay to build houses, while those who live in jungle areas often use wood and leaves. People are very wise, and have used many other things to provide shelter. When wood, rocks and clay are not easily found, then people use a variety of other materials. People in cities use brick and steel to make buildings, while the Inuit of the snowy arctic regions use only snow!



Translation see page 90

Sharks are all of the most feared animals on the planet. For as long as mankind has known about sharks, they have been feared. But actually, sharks pose very little threat to most people. Sharks usually stay away from humans, and only very rarely swim near beaches or other areas with many people. Many scientists believe that when sharks do attack people, it's only because the sharks have mistaken the person for another animal, like a seal. There have been many movies made about sharks, and most show sharks as being vicious and dangerous creatures. But in reality, sharks kill very few people, and overall mankind benefits from their presence in the oceans.



Translation see page 92

Do you believe in ghosts? Many people say that because science hasn't proven that ghosts are real, then they cannot be real. These people say that because there are not any machines or scientific instruments that can help us find ghosts, then they must not be real. But other people have different opinions. These people say that although science can't prove ghosts are real, science also cannot prove ghosts are not real. So there really are two sides to this argument. This is an issue that in the future may never be resolved. But what do you think? Have you ever seen a ghost?



Translation see page 94

Christopher Columbus is one of the most famous explorers in Western history. He was the first European to sail to the Americas. However, he made many mistakes along the way. First of all, he thought he had arrived in India when he had actually arrived in the central American region. For this reason, he called the people of Central America 'Indians'. Also, he got lost all the times. Back in the 15th century, sailors used the stars to steer their ships. Some sailors were very good at this, but Columbus was not. On one occasion, he used the stars to calculate that he was near a certain island in the Caribbean, when actually he was over two thousand kilometers away!



Translation see page 96

# Reading Comprehension Section

I had a very good vacation this summer. In June, just when our school vacation began, my family and I went to Newburyport to visit my grandmother and grandfather. Newburyport is a small town near the ocean. My grandparents have lived there for many years, but it's far from my home, so we can only go to see them a few times each year.

We had a great time with my grandparents. One day we went to the beach and found many seashells and also had fun flying a kite. The next day, my grandfather took my brother and me out in his



Translation see page 99

sailboat. Wow! Sailing is so much fun and my grandfather is a very good sailor. The day after that, we went to a nearby lake to go fishing. My brother caught two big fish, but I didn't catch any. We took the fish home and my grandmother cooked them for dinner. They were delicious!

When we got back from Newburyport, my brother and I went to a summer camp. We stayed there for five days. Every day we did many fun things. We played games, went swimming, told stories, went on walks through the woods, and at night we always had big campfires. This was a very fun summer vacation for me! I hope that my next vacation will be as much fun as this one!



Translation see page 99

13

Dear Lee Qin,

Do you remember me? I'm your old friend James Lee. I haven't written a letter to you in a long time, so I'd like to let you know what I've been doing recently. For the last two years I have been living in the Canadian city of Vancouver. The first year I was here, I was studying English and English literature at the University of Vancouver. It's a very good school and studying there improved my English a lot. When I first arrived in Canada, I found it difficult to communicate with people in English, but now it's no problem.

Most recently, I have been working in an Italian restaurant in downtown Vancouver. My job is to make different kinds of soup and salad. It's a fun



Translation see page 101

job because I get to learn a lot about Italian cooking, and the people I work with are all very nice to me. I only work four days of every week, so I have enough time off to go sightseeing and exploring around Vancouver.

Vancouver is a large city on the West coast of Canada. It's a really beautiful city with many parks, mountains, and even a beach! In the ocean near Vancouver are many islands. I've been to some of them and they're full of natural beauty. All in all, Vancouver is an excellent place and I'm very happy I decided to come here. If you ever feel like coming to Canada, please let me know, because I'd be very happy for you to come visit.

Your Friend,

James Lee



Translation see page 101

14

This Saturday afternoon from 1 pm until 10 pm there will be a Carnival Fun Fair held at the Hillsboro Elementary School on Parker Street in downtown Hillsboro. The fair will include many games, lots of different food to eat, a musical show, as well as many prizes for participants to win.

There will also be a large barbecue cookout beginning at 6 pm and ending when the food is gone! Hamburgers, hot dogs, salad and drinks will all be served free to those who purchase a Carnival Fun Fair entrance ticket. Also the Elvis Rock and Roll Band will give a musical performance beginning at 8 pm and ending when the carnival closes. This performance is also free to all who purchase a Fun



Translation see page 104

Fair ticket.

Tickets for the Carnival Fun Fair cost 5 dollars for adults and 3 dollars for children. All of the money made with the fair will be given to the Hillsboro Elementary School library to purchase new books and a computer. So we hope you can all come out this Saturday for a great time at the Carnival Fun Fair, and also support the Hillsboro Elementary School library. See you there!



Translation see page 104

Dear Mr. Thomas,

How are you? I am not doing very well myself. Do you remember the camera that you let me borrow? Well, I'm sorry to say that there was a little problem and I lost it. Of course, I would like to pay you so that you can buy a new camera, but first I'd like to tell you how I lost it.

Last Friday, the day you lent your camera to me, I went to the beach to look around. It was a nice day, although a little windy. I was walking down the beach taking pictures when I saw a man in a small boat. The man started talking to me and asked if I would like to go for a ride. So I went with him on a short ride.



Translation see page 107

After about twenty minutes, the sun started to set. The sky was orange and red and looked very beautiful. I started to take a picture of the sunset when suddenly a big wave came and hit our little boat! Your camera fell out of my hands into the water, where it sank like a rock. I felt so bad, there was nothing I could do!

So, I am very sorry about losing your camera. I hope you understand that this was an accident. But anyway, please let me know how much it will cost to buy a new one and I'll give you the money at once. I hope that you'll forgive me for this!

Many Apologies,

Jeff Davies



Translation see page 107

Most people know that Americans love cars. Of course, this was not always the case. Up until the 1950s, most Americans relied mainly on trains and busses for transportation. This was because at that time, the average American thought cars were too expensive to buy, maintain, and repair. But this all changed in the 1950s and there are several reasons why.

World War II ended in 1945 and began a time of industrial growth in America. There were many factories and machines left over from the war, and these were changed to create new products. Engineers and factory workers who had experience making weapons during the war started making products for the



Translation see page 109

average American. One thing they started making was cars, and they made them cheaper and better than ever before.

Soon many more Americans were buying the cheaper cars and this caught the government's attention. The government realized that the country needed more and better roads and highways. For many years during the 1950s, the government spent a lot of tax money building new highways to connect all the states, from East to West and North to South. And once Americans saw all these new roads, what did they do? They bought more cars!

Now it is more than fifty years later, and Americans are starting to learn that too many cars on the roads can cause problems. In most cities in America


Translation see page 109

there are too many cars on the roads, and the traffic moves very slowly. Also, cars cause a lot of air pollution, and people are beginning to worry about how this affects environment. For these reasons, many Americans are choosing not to drive cars. So what are they doing instead? They're using trains and busses again!



Translation see page 109

Dear Mr. And Mrs. Lee,

Thank you for your interest in our Tour of America travel package. I would like to give you some more information about our tour and then you will see for yourself why ours is better than the tours offered by other companies.

First of all, our tour takes you to five American cities, while most other tour groups only visit two or three. Our tour will begin in San Francisco in California, then we'll go to Austin, Texas. After two days there, we will travel down to New Orleans in the southern state of Louisiana. From Louisiana, we will go north to the wonderful city of New York.


Translation see page 112

Here you'll get to spend four days shopping, going to museums, and sightseeing around town. Finally, we will go to the midwestern city of Chicago, also known as the 'Windy City.' If you go with a different company, they would only take you to two or three of these places!

The second big advantage of our Tour of America is its size. We limit the size of our travel groups to fifteen people. Why is this? This is so our tour guides can give you better, more personal service. If you have any questions about the places you visit, there will always be a well-informed guide to give you the answer. In other companies, tour groups often have as many as fifty people per group, and this makes it difficult to have your questions answered.



Translation see page 112

So although our Tour of America may be a little more expensive than those offered by other companies, it is definitely worth the extra cost. Please let me know if you have any other questions, and I hope to see you soon on the best Tour of America.

Sincerely,

Thomas Adams

Sunshine Tours of America



Translation see page 112

Computers, televisions, airplanes, and automobiles are all examples of technology that have been developed within the last one hundred years. There is an ongoing argument that many people have about technology and its benefits to society. Most people agree that these machines help us to live easier and more convenient lives. Computers help us do our work faster, televisions can keep us informed, and airplanes and automobiles help us go from one place to another quickly. These are just a few of the advantages of modern technology.

Yet along with these obvious advantages, there are also some disadvantages to consider. Computers are expensive to operate and require that a person spend



Translation see page 115

a lot of time learning how to use them. Sometimes computers can make mistakes and then waste a lot of a person's time. And although televisions are great for getting information out to the public, many people waste too much time watching worthless, meaningless shows. Airplanes and automobiles help people travel faster, but they also cause accidents that kill many people every day.

As is often the case, there are two sides to this argument about technology. On the one hand, technology can make people's lives more efficient and convenient. But on the other hand, technology can also create new problems for people. Both sides of this argument are valid, and it's up to each individual to decide what role technology will play in their own life... and if it's worth it.



Translation see page 115

Chapter

Appendix 附錄

# 這句英文，改變你的人生

## 1

# A fault confessed is halfredressed.

**肯認錯是改過的一半。**

### 故事分享

曾經，歌手優客李林雙人組唱紅了一首聞名大街小巷的成名曲：「認錯」，描述在感情世界中做了錯誤決定，雖想認錯，卻只能追悔的心情。這首歌曲之所以能夠受到大家的喜愛，是因為它真的唱出許多人內心深處的感動。

願意認錯的人，必須放下高傲的自尊，也必須在情緒上，給對方相當程度的彌補與安慰。犧牲自我的認錯，是人際關係中很重要的一種互動。它可以是單純的禮貌，也可以是細心的體貼。當然，它也是做人成敗的重要關鍵。美國總統柯林頓先生當時鬧出桃色緋聞，眾人所指控的，並不是他做了多少荒唐事，而是他有沒有說謊，肯不肯為所做的事負責、道歉。

一家企業訓練員工也是如此。很多人明明犯了錯，卻不認為自己有錯。其實，要做好服務，首先要先勇於認錯。認錯，是出於對自己產品的信心，以及出於對他人的體貼。

因此，一些「消費者如果不滿意購買的物品，七天之內可以無條件退貨」的主張，就是在要求業者能有「勇於認錯」的表現。知名的錄影帶出租業者百事達，一度推出一項促銷活動：「看片若不滿意，免費換片！」。百事達的創意表現十分有趣。內容是這樣的：

一位年輕的女性消費者，她主動的向神父懺悔認錯，她說：「我已經多次去『百事達』租『霸王片』，就是看完片子後，假借各式各樣不滿意的理由，獲得免費換片！千奇百怪的不滿意理由之一是：『為什麼男主角愛的不是我？』」

這支廣告十分幽默，表面看來，是消費者主動向神父告解認錯，精神上，卻是傳達該公司願意向消費者負責的自信心，顯示出百事達的決心：「如果消費者不滿意，那就是我們的錯，所以無條件換片！」

百事達這樣的服務理念，也是「認錯」精神的延伸。有些不懂「認錯」的廠商，因為自己的無知與堅持，平白錯失許多商機。「肯認錯是改過的一半」，只要能夠勇敢認錯，你就能表現出你的優越人格。相反的，假如你還企圖掩飾過錯，恐怕就會更突顯卑下的私心了。

相關諺語

- A fault once denied is twice committed.
  （否認犯錯就是犯錯兩次。）
- A word before is worth two behind.
  （事前一句話，勝過事後兩句話。）
- Least said, soonest mended.
  （愈描愈黑。）

※ 諺語單字補給站

| | | |
|---|---|---|
| **confess** | [kən'fɛs] | 坦白 |
| **redress** | [rɪ'drɛs] | 改正 |
| | | |

## 2

# Heaven helps those who help themselves.

**天助自助者。**

故事分享

很多玩雜技的人，都會耍「兩手三球」。想開始學這個雜技的人，剛開始都會被「接球」這個動作搞得七暈八素。但是，練習久了，他們就會發現想要準確的接到球，不是要修正你「接球」的動作，而是要注意你「拋球」的動作。

只要你拋的韻律對，你就能接到球。拋球是主動，接球是被動。只要主動，你就能創造解決問題的最初的動力。

人生很多事情都是如此。有創造力的人，都會有「主動」這個特質。他們的腦袋不會被鎖死，鐵窗也關不起來，困難也攔阻不了。

美國有一個六十幾歲的老頭，他在一家汽車旅館的附設餐館中上班。他熱愛他的工作，但是，有一天老闆打算把餐館收掉，就給了他二十萬元的退休金。但是他不願意離開熱愛的工作，就留下來繼續經營。但是，兩年之後，錢還是都虧光了。二十萬美金沒了，餐館也沒有了。

老頭有沒有去領救濟金呢？沒有。他也沒有自暴自棄。他覺得自己還年輕，不需要領社會救濟金過活。加上他還有一項「炸雞」的才能。因此，他帶著他獨門特調的麵包粉，和一個鍋子，出門到處賣配方。

經過了22年，他終於成功賣出他的配方，他就是桑德斯上校，肯德基的創始人。在他賣出配方之後五年內，肯德基就拓展了400家分店。到2000年的時候，全球的肯德基餐廳已經超過10000家了。

現在肯德基炸雞那個白白胖胖、樂觀可愛的戴眼鏡老先生，就是桑德斯上校。任何一個想不開的年輕人，都應該到肯德基身邊，想想他的創業歷程。只有「主動」、「主動」、「主動」，積極的朝自己的夢想去努力，你才有機會成就事業。

## 相關諺語

- When you were born, you cried and the world rejoiced. Live your life so that when you die, the world cries and you rejoice.
  （出生時，你哭泣而全世界欣喜。好好過一生，這樣一來，你死時，全世界哭泣而你卻欣喜。）
- We should push our work; the work should not push us.
  （我們應該主動工作，而非被工作推著走。）
- What we do willingly is easy.
  （我們願意做的事情就不覺得難。）
- We must not lie down and cry "God help us."
  （我們不該躺著什麼都不做，只乞求上帝幫助。）
- There is no labor in the labor of love, and there is love in (the) honest labor.
  （做喜愛的事就不覺得苦，踏實的工作孕育出喜愛。）

## ※ 諺語單字補給站

| | | |
|---|---|---|
| **eaven** | [ˈhɛvən] | 上帝 |
| **help** | [hɛlp] | 幫助 |
| **those** | [ðoz] | 那些 |
| **themselves** | [ðəmˈsɛlvz] | 他們自己 |

## 3

# The child is the father of the man.

**少年時代可決定一人之未來。**

### 故事分享

知名的作家也是台大教授的張文亮，他之所以能夠寫出許多科學大師的傳奇故事，就是因為少年時代老師的一句話。一九七三年，張文亮就讀高中三年級時，有一位師範大學的教授到他的學校演講。這位教授演講得相當精彩，演講中，他突然離題說了一句話：「如果要把事情看清楚，就必須回到起初。」

因為這句話，張文亮開始蒐集各個科學大師的成功歷程，了解他們的少年、童年，以及如何成為科學界的一個個里程碑。在他所寫的《回到起初》這本暢銷書中，曾經就提到許多科學大師，是如何在年少年時，就萌發對某一領域的興趣，最後又如何為這個領域產生偉大的貢獻。

《回到起初》這本書籍中的一段威廉森的故事，與張文亮的啟發有相通之處。

圖書館學系在威廉森開始推動之前，是很少人重視的一個科系。因為圖書館老校工的一句話，少年的威廉森開始在圖書館中吸取智慧。

威廉森一向品學兼優，他中學的時候還一度想成為文學家。他熱愛古典文學，喜愛讀書。有一天下課時，威廉森經過老校工的身邊。老校工順口問他：「讀過狄更斯的作品嗎？」當時認定自己以後要當一流文學家的威廉斯，很驚訝的發現，自己竟然從來沒有讀過狄更斯的作品。

威廉森跑到鎮上的圖書館，發現一整排狄更斯的作品，他不知道從何讀起。隔天到了學校，威廉斯馬上詢問老校工：「狄更斯的書很多，不知道從哪裡開始？」老校工說：「從《淒冷之屋》開始讀。」

「The child is the father of the man.」，因為老校工的指引，少年的威廉森聯想到，喜歡讀書和會讀書完全是兩回事。因此他成人之後，雖然唸的是經濟學系，當到經濟學教授，卻一直渴望成立圖書館系。終於，圖書館學系在威廉森的推動之下於一九二六年成立了。

「少年時代可決定一人之未來。」如果我們的少年時代是在充滿熱忱、創意、愛與指引的關懷中成長的，我們的未來一定也能豐富美好。因為，人生就好比堆疊高塔。底層堅固，就不必重頭打地基。穩固的地基，會讓高樓蓋得更高、更穩。

### 相關諺語

- What is learned in the cradle is carried to the grave.
  (幼時所學的東西會帶入墳墓。)
- A young idler, an old beggar.
  (少壯不努力，老大徒傷悲。)
- Age is honorable and youth is noble.
  (長者可敬，少者可貴。)

- Youth does not mind where it sets its foot.
  （年輕人不介意從何處起步。）

※ 諺語單字補給站

| | |
|---|---|
| child [tʃaɪld] | 孩子 |
| father [ˈfɑðɚ] | 父親 |
| | |

## 4

# Every man is his own worst enemy.

**人生最大的敵人是自己。**

### 故事分享

曾經有一個大學生，家境不佳，每天的午餐費用只夠他買一小份肉，還有一份青菜。每次到學校餐廳買午餐，看到同學總是大魚、大肉，他就覺得慚愧，覺得丟臉。不知不覺，他養成了習慣，每天等到餐廳人變少了的時候，才敢去買午餐。

也曾經有一個模特兒，因為前男友為了豐滿的女孩劈腿，背叛了她，從此她對自己的身材很沒信心，即使有代言、表演的機會，她也因為害怕不敢上台，即使是上台了，她卻表現得扭扭捏捏。

人生最大的敵人，何嘗不是自己呢？對失敗的人而言，自己永遠是天天扯自己後腿的那個影子。當成功的機會來臨時，躲在陰影處的負面自我，就會跳出來不斷質疑自己：「你可以嗎？」「你能力那麼差，怎麼做得到呢？」「你別找麻煩了，安分守己做事不就夠了嗎？」

可是，對成功的人來說，自己卻是最可敬的對手。「Every man is his own worst enemy.」這句英文諺語的「worst」原本是指「最糟糕的」，如果改成「worth」，就代表「值得的」。如果想對永遠扯自己後腿的自我來認輸，不如激發自己的潛力，成為一個值得的對手。

諾貝爾獎得主科歇爾，他年僅三十一歲時就為作曲家布拉姆斯開刀治好甲狀腺，但他的成長過程中，卻曾經有一段因為沒認清自我的迷失片段。

出生在瑞士伯恩（Berne）的科歇爾，二十四歲時就取得了醫學博士學位。當時，他認為自己已經學有所成，所以打算拒絕母校慰留他任教的要求，開始掛牌行醫。但是，科歇爾的祖父一聽到這個消息，就立刻從鄉下趕到城市去。因為他的祖父意識到，科歇爾的才智可以幫助整個醫學領域，往更高、更深入的境界來發展。他告訴科歇爾：「你應該趁著年輕，把握一切機會學習，才可能為人類做出更大的貢獻啊！」

科歇爾聽從了祖父的話，回到母校教學，一邊又進行研究，甚至爭取到出國留學的機會，他先後來到柏林、倫敦、巴黎、維也納等地方，向當地的名師虛心求教，繼續鑽研醫學。

不懈的努力，使科歇爾成為首位指出甲狀腺腫瘤與飲食中含碘量有關的人。科歇爾的外科技術使他被譽為是「甲狀腺的外科聖手」。他親自做的甲狀腺手術甚至達到五千例以上。甚至在獲得諾貝爾獎之後，科歇爾也沒有停頓，他發明了治療骨隨炎的新切割方法。

「Every man is his own worst enemy.」人生最大的敵人，就是自己。許多人之所以能夠成功，就是因為他們已經學會迎戰自我，拒絕被自我擊敗，徹底掌握不斷超越自我的能力。

## 相關諺語

- The man who loses his opportunities loses himself.
  (失去機會的人，就是失去了自己。)
- He is only bright that shines by himself.
  (唯有靠自己發光的人，才能真正明亮。)
- You never know what you can do till you try.
  (試了你才知道自己的能耐。)
- You never know till you tried.
  (不試不知。)

### ※ 諺語單字補給站

| |
|---|
| worst [wɝst] 最差的，最不利的 |
| enemy [ˈɛnəmɪ] 敵人，仇敵 |
| opportunity [ˌɑpɚˈtjunətɪ] 機會、良機 |
| |

## Test：對照前面的內容，把單字填入空白處。

1. A (                    ) confessed is half redressed.
   肯認錯是改過的一半。

2. The child is the (                    ) of the man.
   少年時代可決定一人之未來。

3. Every man is his (                    ) worst enemy.
   人生最大的敵人是自己。

## 5

# Between two stools you fall to the ground.

**腳踏雙凳必墜地。**

### 故事分享

腳踏雙凳，就是妥協。世界上很多平庸的立法，平庸的決定，都是出於妥協以及想同時完成兩件事。

假如，比爾．蓋茲的父親對他說：「世界很殘酷，你還是回去先讀完哈佛，然後再去實現理想吧。」如果比爾聽了他父親的話，沒有放棄學業去創業，現在世界上就不會有這樣一位世界首富。

人一旦不是做自己最喜歡的事情，就不會全力以付。結果就造成了平庸。

小利益，往往隱藏著大陷阱。

假如林惠嘉妥協，如果她沒有在李安想學電腦找正職的時候，阻止他說：「不用學了，會電腦的人又不你一個！」假如林惠嘉妥協，現在第一個拿到奧斯卡亞洲人，就未必是李安。

前幾年李安導演的少年PI，又在全球大展雄威，第85屆奧斯卡金像獎入圍十一項，僅次於史蒂芬史匹柏導演的林肯的12項，刷新了李安在奧斯卡的提名記錄，又獲得北卡羅來納影評人協會最佳導演獎，少年PI又獲得金球獎最佳原創音樂獎。

妥協，看起來似乎是最容易的，但是也是最危險的。

《聖經》這本經典書籍中也提過：「心懷二意的人，從神不能得到什麼。」可見專心致力是何等的重要。「Between two stools」站在兩個凳子的中間，你往往找不到著力點，這時候你就容易跌倒，跌到地上之後，不只不容易再站穩，還會弄翻了凳子，變得一無所有。

有一隻狼，牠追著兩隻鹿。一開始牠追著往西方跑去的鹿，往西方跑去的這隻鹿速度很快，一晃眼就不見了，這隻狼突然想到，往東方跑去的那頭鹿似乎腳有點跛，牠趕緊往東方再猛追過去。

這樣一來，這匹狼能夠得到什麼嗎？恐怕什麼都得不到了。這就是「腳踏雙凳」、「心懷二意」最好的註解了。「腳踏雙凳必跌倒」，你想朝某個目標去努力，就得堅持到底。千萬別到了中途又改變方向，最後只能落得一無所獲。

所以，這句諺語可以和「滴水穿石」相呼應。想要不妥協，想要方向恆定，你就需要「堅持的力量」。

相關諺語

- If you run after two hares, you will catch neither.
（同時追兩兔，兩頭都落空。）
- You can't sell the cow and drink the milk.
（魚與熊掌不可兼得。）
- You can't have it both ways.
（事難兩全。）

- A man can't do two things at once.
  （一心不可二用。）
- A man cannot spin and reel at the same time.
  （一個人不能同時紡紗又捲線。）

## 6 Don't count your chickens before they are hatched.

## 勿打如意算盤。

### 故事分享

多年前，股市狂飆的年代，有許多人都把工作辭掉，專心投資股市。

當時，台灣股票市場在一九八九年時已達到上萬點。太多的人在買了股票之後，興奮的看著股市的線型不斷飆升，看著自己手上的股票或者交易存摺，興高采烈的計算自己的資產，很多人曾經一夜之間成為百萬富翁。

打著如意算盤的人，就這麼「看著尚未孵出小雞的雞蛋，啥也不做，光等著小雞出生」。

在那個股市高漲的年代，許多金融公司的經理級人物，隨便分紅就能拿到幾十張、上百張金融股票，每張金融股都三百多元以上，因此他們的身價都上億。

當時，有一家銀行的主管接受當時股價才十幾元的科技公司的邀請，要邀請他去擔任新上市科技公司的財務長。

當時這位金融主管還對科技公司的老闆說：「我們金融股現在的身價那麼高，你們的股價才十幾塊錢，製造的『半導體』又不知道是什麼東西！我如果跳槽到你們公司，不是太笨了嗎？」

誰知道，就在他回絕了科技公司老闆之後，金融股開始狂跌，一路下殺到每股三十元以下。而電子股票卻一路狂漲。因為他拒絕改變，拒絕了解新知，他只願意把所有的雞蛋都放在同一個籃子裡，他錯失了一個絕佳的成功機會。

「Don't count your chickens before they are hatched.」。這句流傳已久的名言，用來形容在股市中認栽的股民，實在是太貼切不過了。

這也是用來提醒投資要小心、謹慎，細心、專注。千萬不要在還沒有收益的時候就貿然又投資，因為你很可能一次就把之前賺的都賠光，還不夠還。

就算你是不投資股市的人或企業，你也需要這句話來提醒自己。為什麼呢? 因為人都是害怕改變，寧可守舊的。

以知名的IBM公司為例。原本這是一家可以繼續在電腦行業執龍頭地位的公司，但是，在80年代的IBM自恃於自己能夠在工業電腦的產業中佔有獨占地位，所以忽略了PC個人電腦（Personal Computer）的重要。

當IBM把PC作業系統的工程外包給微軟公司的時候，這家公司根本沒想到比爾·蓋茲會趁此次機會崛起，並完全扭轉IBM原本的領軍地位。

因此，任何一個掌握成功的人或企業，都該隨時能夠謙卑下來，勿打如意算盤。

面對瞬息萬變的市場與社會，誰能保證自己今天的獲利能夠永遠存在呢？只有在獲利時做好風險評估，才能使自己的地位永遠領先。

## 相關諺語

- Slow and steady/sure wins the race.
  （穩紮穩打，永操勝券。）
- The best is the enemy of the good.
  （「最好」是「好」的敵人。）
- Pride goes before a fall.
  （驕兵必敗。）
- Better an egg today than a hen tomorrow.
  （今日的一顆雞蛋，勝過明天的一隻雞。）

### ※ 諺語單字補給站

| |
|---|
| count [kaʊnt] 數，計算 |
| chicken [ˈtʃɪkɪn] 雞 |
| before [bɪˈfor] 在……之前 |
| hatch [hætʃ] 孵出來 |
| |

## 7

# Don't cross a bridge till you come to it.

## 船到橋頭自然直。

### 故事分享

有一個人因為快艇故障，獨自在外海生存了二十幾天。這二十幾天當中，他靠雨水和飛魚艱苦的維持著生命。好不容易獲救了之後，有人問他內心的感受如何。這個人如此說：「我只要能夠有足夠的食物和足夠的飲水，這一生也就知足了。」

我們是否失去了原本單純知足的心呢？這將使我們憑添許多的煩惱。一個人的憂慮多半是來自於不滿足，有些人在困境還沒有來臨之前就開始憂愁，因為過多憂慮，這樣的人從來不曾好好享受過人生。

過度的憂慮，也會造成一種缺乏自信的危機。美國總統尼克森就是因為缺乏自信，過度憂慮，反而毀掉了自己的政治前途。尼克森總統在1972年時想競選連任，由於尼克森第一任任期時政績斐然，因此很多政治評論家都認為尼克森會獲得壓倒性的勝利。

但是，尼克森本人卻並不這麼想。他走不出過去失敗的內心陰影，因為害怕失敗，他指派手下的人潛入對手總部所在的水門飯店，在對手的辦公室中裝設了竊聽器，事情爆發之後，尼克森還不停阻止調查，拖延處理，推卸責任，就在他選戰獲得勝利後不久，尼克森就因為「水門案」的爆發而被迫辭職。勝券在握的尼克森，最後落得一個羞辱的結果。

「Don't cross a bridge till you come to it.」這句話是用來點醒人們心中的一種常見的習性：「過度憂愁」。其實不僅是個人，公司或者企業，也可能因為太過於憂慮而錯失良機，把賺錢的機會白白的拱手讓人。

有一家上市的企業，每次要有新投資的時候，就會有負面的消息傳過來。逐漸的，這家公司趨於保守，許多投資機會也因此錯失掉了。這家公司好比一隻狼，白天出去找食物。牠經過一戶人家，聽見房中有孩子的哭鬧聲，還有一位老太婆的聲音說著：「別哭啦，再不聽話，就把你扔出去給狼吃！」狼一聽到，心中大喜，就蹲在不遠處等著。太陽下山了，老太婆也沒有把孩子扔出來。

晚上，狼等得不耐煩了，轉到窗戶前想闖入，這時卻聽見老太婆說：「快睡吧，別怕，狼來了，咱們就把它殺死煮了吃。」狼一聽，嚇得一溜煙跑回老窩。同伴問牠收獲如何，牠說：「別提了，老太婆說話不算話，害得我餓了一天，不過幸好後來我跑得快。」

上面那家上市公司所遭遇的困難，就是如此。在市場上，人們關心的是市場博奕，與公司的戰略目標是兩回事，別人信口開河，你就信以為真。卻不知道別人只是拿你當作茶餘飯後的話題。記住，不要讓別人的話，或者自己過度的憂慮，改變了你們公司或你自己的正常運行。因為「Don't cross a bridge till you come to it.」，過度自信和過度憂慮都是一種極端，需要互相平衡，才能冷靜處事。

## 相關諺語

- Don’t worry for tomorrow.
  （不要為明天憂慮。）

- Come what may, heaven won’t fall.
  （無論怎樣，天空都不會掉下來。）

- Don't waste life in doubts and fears.
  （生命不要浪費在猜疑和恐懼中。）

- He who leaves the fame of good works after him does not die.
  （生前做好事，死後留名聲。）

- Misery shows the man what he is.
  （災難使人露出本性。）

- Once a man and twice a child.
  （當一次成人，當兩次小孩。）

- A contented man is always rich.
  （知足的人最富有。）

- Bashfulness is an enemy to poverty.
  （害羞是富裕的敵人。）

- Custom makes all things easy.
  （習慣成自然。）

- Custom is a second nature.
  （習慣是第二天性。）

### ※ 諺語單字補給站

| |
|---|
| cross [krɔs] 越過 |
| bridge [brɪdʒ] 橋 |
| |

## 8

# A little learning is a dangerous thing.

**一知半解最危險。**

### 故事分享

台灣政壇上曾經發生一起震撼社會的事件。那就是2004年總統大選前夕的319槍擊案。這個槍擊案的發生，扭轉了台灣的選舉結果，原本已經民調落後的民進黨候選人陳水扁、呂秀蓮兩人，以一萬多票的差距，勝過了選戰時專打弊案而且民調領先的國民黨候選人連戰、宋楚瑜。

當時，整個社會都相當震撼，敗選陣營的支持者大喊著「當選無效」，國際媒體也大幅報導這次選舉造成的爭議，相關的事件更延續到2006年，造成一連串罷免總統的「倒扁行動」。

整個事件當中，還有一個因為語言認知上的小錯誤而衍伸出的小插曲。

2006年，台北市政府出版的一本中英對照的小冊子中，提到了這個事件，並且使用「drama」這個詞彙來形容這個事件。「drama」中文直譯是「戲劇」的意思，這個用詞引起了許多民眾的抗議與反對，認為這個用詞是不是暗喻總統中槍的事件是在演戲？

然而，在英文裡面，「drama」其實不止「戲劇」一個意義。「drama」可以用來形容一連串的事件，因為319槍擊案後續的發展是一連串的，所以用「drama」來形容並沒有政治涵義，之所以引起大家的抗議與反對，都是因為對英文的正確用法認識不清，一知半解。

一知半解最危險，如果只是對一、兩個名詞的使用錯誤，倒還不算嚴重。但是假如這個名詞涉及人身安全，後果就不堪設想了。

2007年的四月，是台灣地區野生動物大出風頭的一個月。

該月的第一個星期，高雄壽山動物園的鱷魚咬傷了沒有按照標準程序，伸手到籠子裡面打算取出麻醉針的張姓獸醫。當媒體將鱷魚咬著手臂的驚險畫面披露在電視新聞當中時，大家都驚訝的看著這隻兇猛的鱷魚，身上插著兩個麻醉針依然神勇，而鱷魚嘴中的手臂還左、右不停搖晃著。

一般民眾多半只會注意到這個畫面的驚悚。但是，鱷魚專家們卻發現媒體報導有一個失誤之處：這隻據說是尼羅河鱷魚的大鱷魚，身上有不同於尼羅河鱷的黑色斑紋，顯然這並不是尼羅河鱷，而是個性兇猛的河口鱷。

河口鱷又稱為食人鱷，牠性情兇猛，但是動物園居然搞錯了十幾年！而獸醫竟然也不知道這一點細微的差別，還因為不懂得遵照標準程序而被咬斷了手臂。

四月底，海生館的一隻阿根廷陸龜小廷走失了，媒體大幅報導，新聞不斷放播報走失陸龜的模樣。沒想到，又有眼尖的民眾看出這個陸龜並非阿根廷陸龜，而是蘇卡達象龜。海生館趕緊撤下指示牌，然後申請專家鑑定。

從上面兩個例子我們可以知道：世界上最危險的事情，並不是無知，而是一知半解。「A little learning is a dangerous thing.」，飛機維修時，一個技師有可能因為忽略兩種螺絲大小的些微差異，裝了錯誤的螺絲在防風玻璃上，而造成整架飛機墜機；也曾經有美國的的塔台人員，因為語言上的一知半解，認為「Priority」不等於「Emergency」，而沒有讓一台油料用光的飛機優先降落，因此造成墜機，白白斷送幾百條人命。

真正的危險，往往就隱身在這許多一知半解的錯誤當中，所以，你怎麼能不奮力學習呢？

- A little learning is a dangerous thing.
  （一知半解，危險之至。）
- A wise man knows his own ignorance; a fool thinks he knows everything.
  （智者了解自己的無知，愚者以為自己無所不知。）
- Ask a silly question and you'll get a silly answer.
  （問一個愚蠢的問題，你就會得到一個愚蠢的回答。）

- Better to ask the way than go astray.
（多問路不吃虧。）

- Don't claim to know what you don't know.
（不要不懂裝懂。）

- He who asks is a fool for five minutes, but he who does not ask remains a fool forever.
（願意問的人是個五分鐘的傻瓜，不願意問的人是一輩子的傻瓜。）

- Knowledge makes humble, ignorance makes proud.
（博學使人謙虛，無知使人驕傲。）

※ 諺語單字補給站

| |
|---|
| little ['lɪtl̩] 小的，小巧可愛的 |
| learning ['lɝnɪŋ] 學習 |
| dangerous ['dendʒərəs] 危險的，不安全的 |
| |

9

# All men naturally desire to know.

## 人的天性皆欲求知。

### 故事分享

人的天性，天生充滿了求知欲。人總想知道別人所不知道的知識、智慧，人總想尋找機會學習得更多。

仔細翻閱各國的歷史文獻，我們會發現，即使是幼兒，也能夠熱愛閱讀。而且，凡是提早教幼兒閱讀的，幾乎都有很高的成效。幼兒的求知欲是天生的，人的天性皆是充滿好奇心的！

曾經有一家幼稚園的女教師，她在提交的一份報告中指出：有一次她對班級裡的學生們講一本新的故事書時，有一個五歲的幼兒，堅持說要自己看這本書。女老師告訴他：「這是一本大家都還沒看過的新書。」

但是五歲的小朋友堅持說，他能夠讀懂這本書，他想要自己看。女老師為了讓他死心，就決定讓他試試看，於是把書交給他。沒想到，這個五歲的小孩子，竟然對著全班同學，很流暢的把這本書從頭到尾讀完了。

像這種例子似乎越來越多。台灣的媒體就曾經大幅報導過一個三歲的幼童，居然能夠朗朗背誦諸如：《弟子規》、《孝經》、《三字經》等等著名經典，而且如果他母親不讓他背誦，他還會鬧脾氣呢！其實，幼兒從整個社會、環境，還有所有的人，學會說話及閱讀。因為他們能夠透過閱讀電視、電影的字幕，透過把玩家裡的廣告、郵件、DM、玩具標章、道路招牌，學習說話、閱讀。對幼兒來說，這些環境都是幼兒的老師。

張炘陽，一個十歲就成為大學生的天才兒童，他的父親張會祥，就曾經在《神奇的學習》一書中分享到他教育張炘陽的經過：

「他不到三個月的時候，我們買了軍棋、象棋等玩具。我用這些玩具和他玩兒，誰知道，我說『當頭炮』，他就拿起『炮』，我就覺得奇怪，這孩子識字，還是記住了什麼方法了呢？後來，我就慢慢教他幾個字，結果孩子學得非常快。每教了一個字，我就拿一本筆記本寫上去，之後還進行分類。教他字的時候，我也不是按照課本那樣，正正經經的教，有時候，我拿起一個煙盒，就把煙盒上面的字教給他知道。到了炘陽三個月的時候，他就已經學會兩千字了。」

張炘陽成功的例子和張爸爸的分享，啟示我們：只要能滿足兒童的求知欲，不加以限制，他們就能達到讓人驚訝的成功境界。

## 相關諺語

- All men naturally desire to know.
  （人生而有求知欲。—亞里斯多德）
- As we live, so we learn.
  （我們活著，所以我們學習。）

- Men's natures are all alike; it is their habits that carry them far apart.
  (性相近，習相遠。)

※ 諺語單字補給站

| naturally [ˈnætʃərəlɪ] 天生的 |
| --- |
| desire [dɪˈzaɪr] 渴望 |
| know [no] 知道、瞭解 |
| |

英語系列：27

# 英語閱讀滿分特訓

主編／施銘瑋
作者／ Craig Sorenson
譯者／林靜慧
出版者／哈福企業有限公司
地址／新北市中和區景新街 347 號 11 樓之 6
電話／(02) 2945-6285　傳真／(02) 2945-6986
郵政劃撥／ 31598840　戶名／哈福企業有限公司
出版日期／ 2016 年 4 月
定價／ NT$ 249 元 (附 MP3)

全球華文國際市場總代理／采舍國際有限公司
地址／新北市中和區中山路 2 段 366 巷 10 號 3 樓
電話／(02) 8245-8786　傳真／(02) 8245-8718
網址／ www.silkbook.com　新絲路華文網

香港澳門總經銷／和平圖書有限公司
地址／香港柴灣嘉業街 12 號百樂門大廈 17 樓
電話／(852) 2804-6687　傳真／(852) 2804-6409
定價／港幣 83 元 (附 MP3)

視覺設計／ Wan Wan
內文排版／ Jo Jo
email ／ haanet68@Gmail.com

郵撥打九折，郵撥未滿 500 元，酌收 1 成運費，
滿 500 元以上者免運費



國家圖書館出版品預行編目資料

英語閱讀滿分特訓 / 施銘瑋◎主編 Craig Sorenson◎ 著
.林靜慧◎譯 -- 新北市：哈福企業, 2016.04
面； 公分. -- (英語系列；27)
ISBN 978-986-5616-52-6(平裝附光碟片)

1.英語 2.讀本

805.18　　105003907

哈福

哈福